"YOU ARE ALL VOLUNTEERS IN THE ARMY OF THE RIGHTFUL DESTINY.

First you will be outfitted in proper uniform, be issued weapons, given your training assignments, and be initiated into basic training."

"Told you," Croft muttered out of the side of his mouth.

"Give up all your scumlike cowardly instincts. You are now warriors and will behave like warriors. Anything less will be considered treason. Some of you have obviously had experience in warfare. Your puny skills may do you some good in survival, but you must adopt our ways of combat. And you will.

"You will remember that this is war! *This is war!* Every fiber of your being, every muscle in your body, every synapse in your brain will now be devoted to war!"

Berkley Battlestar Galactica Books

BATTLESTAR GALACTICA
by Glen A. Larson and Robert Thurston

BATTLESTAR GALACTICA 2: THE CYLON DEATH
MACHINE
by Glen A. Larson and Robert Thurston

BATTLESTAR GALACTICA 3: THE TOMBS OF KOBOL
by Glen A. Larson and Robert Thurston

BATTLESTAR GALACTICA 4: THE YOUNG WARRIORS
by Glen A. Larson and Robert Thurston

BATTLESTAR GALACTICA 5: GALACTICA DISCOVERS
EARTH
by Glen A. Larson and Michael Resnick

BATTLESTAR GALACTICA 6: THE LIVING LEGEND
by Glen A. Larson and Nicholas Yermakov

BATTLESTAR GALACTICA 7: WAR OF THE GODS
by Glen A. Larson and Nicholas Yermakov

BATTLESTAR GALACTICA 8: GREETINGS FROM EARTH
by Glen A. Larson and Ron Goulart

BATTLESTAR GALACTICA 9: EXPERIMENT IN TERRA
by Glen A. Larson and Ron Goulart

BATTLESTAR GALACTICA 10: THE LONG PATROL
by Glen A. Larson and Ron Goulart

BATTLESTAR GALACTICA 11: THE NIGHTMARE MACHINE
by Glen A. Larson and Robert Thurston

BATTLESTAR GALACTICA 12: "DIE, CHAMELEON!"
by Glen A. Larson and Robert Thurston

BATTLESTAR GALACTICA 13: APOLLO'S WAR
by Glen A. Larson and Robert Thurston

BattlestaR GALACTICA 13

APOLLO'S WAR

APOLLO'S WAR
Novel by Glen A. Larson and Robert Thurston
Based on the Universal Television Series
"BATTLESTAR GALACTICA"
Created by Glen A. Larson

B®

BERKLEY BOOKS, NEW YORK

BATTLESTAR GALACTICA 13:
APOLLO'S WAR

A Berkley Book/published by arrangement with
MCA PUBLISHING RIGHTS, a Division of MCA, Inc.

PRINTING HISTORY
Berkley edition/January 1987

ISBN: 0-425-09476-6

A BERKLEY BOOK ® TM 757,375
Berkley Books are published by the Berkley Publishing Group,
200 Madison Avenue, New York, N.Y. 10016.
The name "Berkley" and the stylized "B" with design
are trademarks belonging to Berkley Publishing Corporation.
PRINTED IN THE UNITED STATES OF AMERICA

To Jason

And to Robert Fox, "Ace of Aces,"
And the Indomitable Members of
the Little Ferry "Flying Foxes" Squadron

PART I

CHAPTER ONE

Like all insects of Yevra, the rock beetles were a hardy species whose lineage went back more generations than any other kind of living creature on the planet. There had even been rock beetles in the prehistory of Yevra, tiny early versions of the insect that had, even then, blended in with their geological surroundings. Later, when other primitive creatures roamed the planet's surfaces, rock beetles had grown larger and more intelligent. They had begun to communicate in simple ways, using their antennae for signals, discovering a kind of rockbound dance that allowed them to display the mating urge, dispatching from glands a pheromonal secretion that located objects for their mating urge, receiving sound vibrations through the tiny spines, or sensilla, upon their bodies. The present-day Yevran rock beetle is often larger than an average human foot. Fortunately, for them and anyone observing them, their chameleonic ability to change the surface of their bodies to match the coloring of rocks made them virtually invisible. The only inhabitants of Yevra who knew of the whereabouts of an individual rock beetle were other rock beetles.

The gray-speckled one that now perched on a high gray speckled rock was unmoving, intent on receiving the information that came through the air from others of his species. Modern-day rock beetles communicated in a language of intricate sounds created by chewing motions in their crooked mouths and by the tapping of their stiff wings against each other. The wings were rarely used for flying and, anyway, a rock beetle could only fly a short distance at best. Most stayed in one small area during their lives, moving around only when they needed to feast on the smaller insects beneath the rocks. Sounds were received on mechanoreceptors, touch cells containing thin tactile hairs which responded to the sound and sent messages by nerve impulses to the brain. Except for messages about food and mating, most communication among the rock beetles dealt with significant changes in their environment.

Such a change had just been witnessed by the gray-speckled rock beetle. Coordinating the varied images in his multifaceted compound eyes, he detected a new presence in the sky above him. It was either a three-sectioned being or perhaps three very large birds. He sent the message out, and it was carried quickly along the network of individual rock beetles scattered among many rocks. Quick analyses were made and it was agreed that it must either be a trio of birds or some new kind of creature.

The speckled beetle watched the oddity above him grow even larger. He could see now that it was indeed three separate entities and he started that information out on its path along the network. The three things flew over the speckled beetle, made long sweeping turns and quickly lowered themselves to the ground. A breeze seemed to come out of nowhere and stir up dust swirls as they landed. They came to a stop. The beetle waited for them to start walking along, searching for whatever had brought them down from the skies. And then, what appeared to be the eyes of the new creatures split open with a sharp crackling sound. Before the beetle could send this new occurrence along the network, smaller creatures emerged from the new opening. The beetle recognized at once that these newcomers looked like other creatures which he'd seen pass by his rock at rare times—humanoid creatures. Sunlight reflected off large objects which they held in their hands.

Apollo held his flight helmet in his hand as he stepped out of his Viper. As soon as he hit ground, he tossed it back into the cockpit. Sheba and Croft stepped onto Yevran ground suspiciously. Croft wrinkled his nose in distaste.

"You absolutely sure this air is breathable, Apollo?" he said. His craggy face was fixed in that almost permanent look of cynicism that had become his trademark. The look, along with the aggressive way he held himself, tended to make people steer clear of him when he was in a bad mood. He was often in a bad mood.

Apollo's look was a definite contrast to Croft's. Even when he was serious or troubled, kindness never left his clear blue eyes. Those who knew him well realized that, if prodded, he could become quite fierce with fury, but he did not, like Croft, wear his anger like a battle jacket.

"According to the atmospheric analyzer," Apollo informed Croft, "this planet checks out as .82 equivalent of our air, with no poison gases or—"

"Okay, okay, I get the point. Analyzer doesn't analyze how much a place stinks, I guess. This reminds me of dry rot in a detox chamber."

Sheba, getting a clear sensory memory of the odors inside a detox chamber, frowned and shuddered. With her helmet off, her long dark-brown hair draped onto the shoulders of her flight jacket and seemed to emphasize her body's long and thin lines.

"Let's look around," Apollo said.

"From what I saw coming in, what we see here is just like the rest of the damn place," Croft said.

"Don't you ever get optimistic, Croft?" Sheba asked as they began their slow and careful exploration of the immediate area.

"Not if I can help it. Optimism means danger, far as I'm concerned."

Sheba's natural wide-eyed look became even wider as she gave Croft a puzzled look.

"You'll have to run that by me again," she said.

After making sure that nothing repulsive or malevolent cluttered the surface of a high nearby rock, Croft sat on it. As it happened, he nearly squashed the gray-speckled rock beetle who had been tracking the movement of the three warriors from the *Battlestar Galactica*. The beetle scurried out of the way, into a niche in the rock. Croft did not detect its movement.

"I look at it this way," he said. "See, if I'm optimistic about convincing you to make love to me, I get disappointed and will probably make mistakes. Pessimism tells me my chances are low. Makes me try harder. Makes the game more interesting."

Sheba smiled. Croft noted that, with her large eyes and thin wide mouth, both emphasized by her smile, Sheba sometimes looked strange to him. Not even pretty. Yet, he dreamed about her almost every night. He often wondered why he had this preoccupation with a female he could not win. Then she would turn a certain way and look so lovely he lost his breath and couldn't stand to look at her.

"Either way, optimism, pessimism, you don't get me."

Her words hurt him more than he showed, but he kept his voice carefully cynical: "Don't be so sure of that, lovely. I can see how I'm breaking down your resistance centon by centon."

He saddened as he saw Sheba glance longingly toward Apollo. The woman's interest clearly lay in that direction, just like that of most of the available women on the *Galactica*. Apollo, with his sharply defined good looks and his image as a hero, was a real heartthrob all right. A real heartbreaker, too, who didn't even seem to notice the sad loving glances of the women he passed. Since the death of his mate, Serina, not long after they had been sealed in a wedding ceremony, Apollo's attentions to the Galactican women had been rare. Croft had heard a rumor that Sheba and Apollo had been an item for a brief time, but he'd never been able to verify it.

Apollo, who had been exploring a nearby area, came back to Croft and Sheba.

"Can we take a look around now?" he asked, an edge of sarcasm in his voice. "That is, if you two have finished your discussion."

Croft hated the way Apollo's words brought a miserable look to Sheba's face, and he wanted to tell him off and pop him one.

"Don't be touchy, Captain," Croft said.

The slight narrowing of his eyelids might not have been recognized as a wince except by people who knew Apollo. Croft spotted the eyelid movement easily, and he smiled. He usually called Apollo "Captain" just to annoy him. Besides, it pointed up the odd discrepancy in their ranks. As a commander, Croft should have outranked Apollo, but both men knew that the commandership was only honorary, an old rank reinstated by Commander Adama merely to reward Croft for his heroism in the mission to destroy the massive laser cannon on the ice planet Tairac. Before that, he'd been a convict on the fleet's prison ship, the grid barge. After he'd been restored to rank, Croft had been given the helm of the grid barge, a position he hated. He took every opportunity to get away from the barge and on patrols, even routine patrols like this one. But Apollo was in charge, on this mission and on any other he took out. Croft couldn't pull rank because this captain was Commander Adama's son, the wedge that gave him all the power he needed. Power he took, in spite of his protests to the contrary.

The rock beetle kept watch on the three Galactican warriors exploring the immediate area. When they passed out of his vision, he heard more about their wanderings through the communication network of fellow beetles. The dark brown beetle that now watched them was on a rock the same color. From his insect point of view the humans were enormous. As they went by him, he transmitted his vision of them back to the gray-speckled rock beetle.

Sheba stopped to scan the horizon.

"Doesn't look too promising, this place, does it?" she said.

"Nope," Apollo answered. "But the situation's too crucial. We have to check every planet within range of the fleet."

"While using up fuel as we do so," Croft commented. "Not a practical solution."

"But the only solution, Croft."

"Aye, aye, Captain."

The overall fuel and supply situation for the *Galactica* and the ragtag fleet had recently become critical. The ships had been traveling a long while without discovering any new places to refuel and restock. Throughout the fleet, fuel levels were generally low, without sufficient reserve. Some of the ships were being piggybacked, a fleet term describing the pulling along of one ship by another, more powerful one. Supplies were being severely rationed.

When Apollo, Croft and Sheba had left, a potent political situation aboard the *Galactica* itself had been growing. Crews from other ships had sent representatives to the Council of Twelve meeting on the *Galactica* to complain about inequities. They claimed that the people of the command ship had too many privileges, that they were somehow excused from the deprivations experienced by others. There was an iota of truth in the belief, but it had nothing to do with elite privileges. Commander Adama had indeed ordered extra rations for any pilots going out on patrol, but no other officers received any such advantages. The pilots had earned these privileges because they were doing the harrowing and exhausting job of searching one barren planet after another for fuel or supplies. Before Apollo's patrol had left the ship, there had been news that a patrol led by Lieutenant Starbuck had landed on a planet that looked promising. However, Apollo's patrol, on a strict schedule, had not been able to hang around the ship to hear the results of Starbuck's mission.

"Did you broadcast back our coordinates to the *Galactica*, Croft?" Apollo asked.

"Tried."

Apollo whirled around, irritated by Croft's lackadaisical reply.

"What do you mean, tried?"

"Your grasp of language failing, Captain? I said I tried. We're out of immediate range of the coded communication channels, and Adama specifically ordered us not to—"

"Yes, I see. But they'll be able to track us if they have to, based on our last reported coordinates."

"Perhaps."

Apollo turned away, in order to ignore Croft's mild sneer. The antagonism between him and Croft had increased recently. There had been a brief period when they had almost approached friendship, after they had worked and fought together closely to free the enslaved civilization on a planet whose alien name translated as "The Joyful Land." A camaraderie had developed between them there that hadn't been duplicated on any task or mission they had performed together since their return to the fleet. Croft seemed to thrive on their rivalry, but Apollo hated it. He had never liked to be at odds with any other human being, and especially those he had to work with.

Neither man had been originally scheduled for this mission. Croft had volunteered when Lieutenant Jolly became ill, and Apollo had replaced the exhausted Ensign Greenbean. Doctor Salik had ordered bedrest for Greenbean. Apollo didn't mind going out. Since he had become flight coordinator for the *Galactica*, he had had fewer opportunities to fly the routine patrols. He liked the patrols, or any excuse to sail through space in his swift Viper. Croft resented Apollo's appointment as flight coordinator. He saw it as another instance of command nepotism, and he had sarcastically referred to it a couple of times during the present mission.

After they had traveled some distance, seeing nothing but more barren landscape, Croft commented: "I think we can pass on this godforsaken place."

"I'm inclined to agree. Let's just check over this next rise, then go back."

"Right beside you."

The three warriors strode forward. As they came to the top of a hill, Apollo felt a wave go through his body. It seemed like an electrical charge or an energy impulse, but it had passed through too quickly for him to interpret it. Ahead of him some rocks seemed to glow. Could the wave have come from these new rocks? Why was he beginning to feel dizzy?

A somewhat distorted picture of Apollo as he swayed from dizziness was being watched on a long narrow screen by two lizardlike beings in military uniforms. One was clearly an officer, as the amount of ornate metallic finery on his black and gray uniform attested, and the other, who sat at the screen and wore a much plainer version of the uniform, was clearly a subordinate. Although both had a well-defined reptilian look, they were in most respects humanoid. With an only slightly bent spine, they stood upright on legs which almost exactly duplicated the bone structure of human legs. Their arms had an extra joint which gave their movements a sinuous effect, and their hands had four fingers which they could spread widely. Underneath their uniform sleeves one might have been surprised by the many tiny spines all over the skin of their arms. The green tinge of their scaly skins might have convinced most humanoids to classify them in a different biological order, but technically they *were* humanoid.

The subordinate had been observing the pilots from the *Galactica* ever since a scanner had detected their Vipers' presence in the skies. The officer had just been summoned to the screen.

"They appear to be prime prospects for us," the officer said. He had no nose, and his nostrils vibrated when he spoke.

"I agree, sir," the subordinate said.

"How came they here?"

The subordinate worked controls at the side of the console, and onscreen the trio of Vipers appeared. The officer studied the vehicles.

"Sophisticated craft, do you think?" he said.

"Yes, sir."

"They appear to be extremely high-powered. I suspect these beings came from far off, like the last group we discovered. Perhaps, with all these visitors, we can learn how to escape from this sector with such power. The craft will be worth studying at any rate."

"I take it then, sir, that we will accept these beings into our ranks."

"I believe we will. They are clearly humanoid. Humanoids have proven useful fighters for us in the past, don't you agree?"

"Agreed, sir."

"Good. When they have separated enough for us to warp them in separate beams, activate the trap and bring them through the force field."

"Yes, sir."

"Then we will also capture and transport their powerful vehicles."

"Very good, sir."

"Assign a noncom to further observation of them, and eventual recruitment."

"Yes, sir."

They continued to gaze at the screen until the officer gave the order to trap the newcomers.

Apollo tried to shake the dizziness out of his head. He stumbled forward. Sheba took a couple of steps toward him. He waved her away.

"Apollo," she said, "is there anything wrong?"

"Nothing."

Unconvinced, she wanted to rush to him, touch him, help him, but he tended to reject sympathy, or even simple compassion, from her or anyone else. Sheba wished she could get emotionally closer to the stoic captain, but he had discouraged all her overtures, especially since that brief time when they had been romantically involved.

Apollo swayed again and blinked his eyes several times. Sheba began to feel a bit woozy herself. She glanced toward Croft, who seemed to be fading out. She blinked her own eyes. Was this a trick of vision, something gone wrong with her eyes? No, Croft was *really* fading out. She took a step, stumbled.

"What's going on?" she cried.

Apollo fell. As he became unconscious, he saw half of Sheba disappear.

The rock beetle, seeing the scene through the multiple eyes of another beetle along the communication network, watched the three human beings shimmer slightly before vanishing. Each one appeared to rise a short distance in the air before being lost to insect vision. He had seen such magical events before, with different kinds of creatures, all of whom, when they reached that section of ground, disappeared. Some of their own kind had also disappeared, and sent back no messages. Another message came from another line of the communication network: the strange shells the human beings had arrived in had also vanished.

CHAPTER TWO

Surveying the activity on the *Galactica* bridge from his favorite observation point, right next to the starfield window, Tigh thought: *It's as busy here as a herd of wild daggits on a rampage*. At least half of the bridge crew was engaged in guiding Starbuck's squadron toward its landing. The rest were preparing to dispatch the group of shuttles and cargo ships whose job it would be to evaluate the riches, or lack of them, on the apparently fruitful planet the squadron had discovered. Commander Adama glanced toward Tigh with that expression which his old friend and executive officer recognized as the need for a report. Tigh immediately strode to Adama's side, saying, "This one feels right, sir."

Adama nodded.

"Yes, Tigh, I agree. The data Starbuck transmitted ahead seems to indicate rich sources of fuel and food for the fleet."

As usual, Tigh was amused by the careful wording of the commander's comment. Adama was famous throughout the ship for hiding his optimism behind a meticulously cautious vocabulary.

"Any word from Apollo and his squadron?" Adama asked.

Tigh matched Adama's caution with his own carefully chosen words.

"Nothing yet. They went beyond coded channel range. I'm sure they'll communicate momentarily."

"Momentarily?"

"Well, they are twenty centons overdue for their next report."

They stared at each other for a moment. However wary their words, each could see the deep concern in the other's eyes. Tigh, eager to keep Adama from unnecessary worrying, said softly, "Perhaps they've discovered something significant and are checking their data before reporting in."

Adama's eyes clearly showed he was not convinced.

"Perhaps."

The two men turned their attention to normal routine. When all the Vipers of Starbuck's squadron were safely landed, half of the bridge crew instantly relaxed.

Moments later Starbuck dutifully reported in to the commander. Adama listened quietly as the young lieutenant supplied the hopeful information about the planet his squadron had found. As Starbuck spoke, Adama's daughter, Athena, in charge of operations for the shift, joined the two men. When Starbuck was finished, Adama grasped his shoulders firmly and said, "Good job, Lieutenant."

Starbuck, his handsome face reddening just a little, was obviously pleased. As he brushed back the usual unruly strands of his straw-colored hair, he said crisply, "Thank you sir." He took a step backward but, before turning, he addressed Adama again. "Sir? They told me, down at landing bay, that Apollo, Croft and Sheba haven't returned yet."

"That is correct, Starbuck."

"Is everything all right?"

"We have to assume that until . . ."

"Until what?"

"Until we know that it isn't all right."

Both Starbuck and Athena flinched at that declaration. Flight Officer Omega brought Adama some new data about the ships to be launched. As Adama attended to them, Athena whispered quietly to Starbuck, "Apollo's all right. No problem. He'll be reporting in any moment."

Starbuck's voice dropped to a whisper.

"You feel it, too, don't you?" he said.

"Feel what?"

"That something's wrong. I always know when something's wrong with Apollo. So do you. He's too methodical. He wouldn't allow that long a period of time to pass before a scheduled report, unless something *was* wrong."

Her eyes saddening, Athena nodded. Starbuck noticed Adama's shoulders slump as he listened to Omega. He rushed to the commander, with Athena only a step behind him.

"What's wrong, sir?" he said.

Tigh, who had also noted the change in Adama's body, rushed up. Adama tried to wave both Starbuck and Tigh away. Omega turned to the two men and said, "I had the Vipers of Captain Apollo's squadron on-scan briefly, then they disappeared."

"Disappeared?" Starbuck said.

"How briefly, Omega?" Athena asked.

"Not long. Just a micron or two. If I hadn't been searching for them, I'd never have noticed. They were there, a couple of flashes, they were gone. That's what it looked like. Like they just flashed out of existence."

"Don't panic," Adama said, struggling to keep his voice calm. "It was merely their ships. They might not have been in them."

"They seemed to be flying over some kind of terrain just before they blipped out."

"Do you have the coordinates, Omega?" Starbuck said.

"Not established, lieutenant. We have the sub-sector, but nothing more."

"Then we'll have to search every damn planet in the damn sub-sector."

Starbuck appeared ready to initiate search procedures right that moment.

"Starbuck," Tigh said, "that area's positively dense with star systems. There must be more than two hundred planets, and uncountable asteroids, and—"

"Tigh, we've got to do something!"

Starbuck's desperate plea silenced the bridge. Everyone stared at each other. When Adama spoke in a whisper, his words could be heard everywhere in the immense chamber: "We will do something. We'll send out the routine search party."

Starbuck whirled around and faced his commander angrily.

"Routine? Just routine. Commander, this calls for an extensive scouring pattern, the integration of all our available craft into—"

"Simmer down, Lieutenant. Taking over command of the *Galactica*, are you?"

The characteristically hot-tempered Starbuck was tempted to say yes.

"No, sir, but—"

"No buts, Starbuck. Captain Apollo wouldn't want us to commit so many of our vehicles to a simple search for a lost patrol. Especially when there is so much work to be done on the planet you and your squadron discovered. Especially when our fuel levels are already at crisis points."

"But, sir, this is Apollo, your—"

Staring into Adama's steely eyes, Starbuck found he couldn't articulate the word *son*. The comment would have been insubordinate as well as insulting. Instead, he merely stuttered and went silent. Adama turned toward his executive officer.

"Colonel Tigh, assemble a search party and order them to deploy in arachnid pattern over the sub-sector. Use full instrumentation and report all anomalies, no matter how insignificant they may seem."

Running off, Tigh shouted back, "Yes, sir," as he immediately set about implementing the orders.

His body going slack, Adama glanced toward Starbuck and Athena, each of whom appeared hostile and angry. No wonder. They were agonizing over the loss of a friend and brother, and could not understand his strict attention to duty. He wanted to commit more vehicles. He even wished to join the search party himself. But responsibility outweighed all personal feelings. Adama's responsibility was to the *Galactica* and to the fleet. Apollo was only one man; there were hundreds of thousands of people under Adama's care. His son would have demanded that nothing be done to jeopardize the welfare of the people. He could almost hear Apollo saying to send no more ships after him than regulations called for. He hated even the slightest element of favoritism bestowed upon him by his father.

The last time Adama had talked with his son, just before the current mission, they had had one of their tiffs. These little arguments had been coming with increasing frequency as Apollo became more and more burdened with the responsibility of command. The skin around Apollo's eyes had become dark from sleeplessness, from the extra tours of duty he pushed on himself so stubbornly. His mouth had hardened into a thin, grim line ever since the death of his wife Serina during the battle on the planet Kobol. Even when he smiled, there was a hint of sadness in his eyes. When he laughed, there was a hollow sound just beneath the laughter.

Their argument had been about some technical detail or other. Adama recalled something about Viper deployment on missions. Whatever it had been, Apollo had become irritated. He suggested that his father's tactical concepts did not apply to their current situation. He said something about them being buried back in space academy texts. Adama had become angry and a little sarcastic, and soon they were in a shouting match. And all over a few technical details. They had both calmed down but had parted with some tension still hanging between them.

"Commander Adama?" Starbuck asked.

Adama blinked away his reverie. Seeing the frustration in Starbuck's eyes, he spoke to the brash young lieutenant sternly.

"Consider your words before you speak them, Starbuck."

"I have, sir. I wish to lead the search party."

"Starbuck, you've just come off a long, tiring flight. You need your rest."

"Negative, sir. I wouldn't be able to rest, not until Apollo is found or we have exhausted every resource to—to—"

He couldn't say it, couldn't admit the possibility that Apollo might not be found. Adama nodded, releasing Starbuck from the obligation of finishing the sentence.

"Permission granted, Lieutenant Starbuck. Report to Colonel Tigh for briefing."

"Thank you, sir."

Starbuck turned briskly on his heel and strode off the bridge. Athena hugged her father's arm, put her head against his shoulder. He patted her hand.

"We'll find him, I know," Athena whispered.

"He may report in any moment," Adama said, the certainty of his words not matched by what he felt inside.

"Exactly."

"There are things I should have said to him, Athena, things—"

"Hush. He knows. We both know."

Adama smiled at his daughter's comforting words but, no matter how much he tried to put the picture out of his head, he still recalled the stern look on his son's face when Adama had last seen him.

Apollo dreamt of his father's face, looking sternly at his own stern face. At their last meeting, Apollo had merely turned and left the room. In the dream, he started to go, then whirled around, rushed to his father and hugged him. They rarely hugged. Now, even in the dream, he could feel his father's strong grip. Then the grip dissolved along with his father's appearance into a bright white light. Apollo felt heat just underneath his eyelids, the heat of a sun. He came awake suddenly and realized he was lying on his back. The heat and light came from the sun in the sky above him. He opened his eyes and quickly averted them from the brightness. When his vision cleared, he saw a clump of grass beside his head. Its blades were a vivid deep green with flecks of red at the base.

Slowly he remembered landing on a planet, exploring, getting dizzy, blanking out. He sat up, saw he was quite alone. This meadow was nothing like the barren stretch of ground they'd been exploring. It was lush and attractive, with complex tangles of greenery that seemed to embrace and even strangle exotic red, yellow and purple flowers, with short soft grass, with tall impressive trees.

Standing up, he examined himself. He was no longer in the uniform of the *Battlestar Galactica*. He now wore a jacket of stiff material, with no collar and an uneven raggedy hem. His plain trousers were of similar cloth. On his feet sandals had replaced his flight boots. His jacket was tucked at the waist by a wide belt which had a set of strange-looking shiny metal studs all around it. The material of these strange new clothes made his skin itch. Without thinking about it, he reached inside his jacket and absentmindedly scratched the skin of his chest.

Speaking out loud, he tried to collect his thoughts.

"I was walking through a rocky place—that's right, a rocky place. I felt dizzy. Then I blacked out. Now I'm here. How

did I get here? Where is this? Where's Sheba? Croft? The
Vipers, where are they?''

He began to walk around, studying the vegetation. What a
lovely place this seemed to be, so suitable for human life, for
all kinds of life. Their telemetry had indicated nothing like this
when they had landed on the planet. Was he on a different
planet now? Had he somehow been transported elsewhere?

He thought he saw movement near a tree. When he went
closer, he saw nothing. However, he felt a strange warmth at
his waist. Looking down, he saw that one of the studs on his
belt had lighted up. Reaching down, he touched the glowing
stud. It began to emit a low humming sound. With a series of
gentle tugs, the belt seemed to be urging Apollo to walk forward. He followed the impulse, took a few steps into the woods.
The pull became stronger. He tried to resist it and could not.
There was nothing he could do but continue in the direction it
led him. He became more alert than ever, flexing his fingers
readily. If he encountered anything, he had no weapon. He'd
have to fight his way out.

Suddenly the pull ceased. Looking down, he saw a small
furry animal, sitting at his feet. Apollo sat on his haunches and
stared at the tiny creature. It had tiny pointed ears and a long
rodentlike snout. Its arms, held stiffly at its sides, were thin
and furry only in patches. He wondered why it didn't move,
run away. He stared at its eyes, which were glazed. They looked
like buttons placed in eye sockets. Perhaps it was dead. He
reached out and touched it. While the creature didn't react to
the touch, Apollo noted that it gave off strong body heat. It
was clearly alive, but in some way hypnotized. Well, no reason
to disturb it further, he thought. He stood up and started to
walk away. The pull from the belt resumed. It would not allow
him to walk more than three steps, then it firmly edged him
back toward the small animal. Apollo tried to resist, but only
stumbled. He pressed the button he'd touched before. The light
and hum went out. Life suddenly returned to the animal's eyes.
It stared up, frightened, at Apollo. It appeared about to run
off, but a man jumped out from behind a nearby tree and
pounced on it. He picked the animal up, his mouth wide open,
revealing rotted teeth. Apollo saw he intended to bite the animal's throat.

"Hey!" Apollo shouted. "What—"

He made a grab for the animal, but it was too late. Blood gushed out of the animal's throat as the man bit into it. Angry, Apollo made a move toward the man, who backed away, his eyes as scared as the animal's had been. He flung the dying creature at Apollo, who stepped aside as it brushed past him, leaving a few small bloodstains on his trousers.

"I thought you didn't want it," the man yelled.

"Want it?" Apollo asked. "For what?"

"For your meal."

"My meal? I don't—"

The man turned and skittered away into the darkness of the woods before Apollo could finish his sentence. He walked to the dead animal and knelt by it. The blood had stopped gushing from its throat. Its eyes were now glazed for good. He scooped some dirt over it. The idea of eating the animal had sickened him. He had to get away from this spot. As he walked, a long time passed before he could get the smell of the animal's blood out of his nose.

CHAPTER THREE

His name was unknown to anyone on Yevra. On the planet he came from, he belonged to a religious cult whose members' names were kept secret from anyone outside the cult. He had left his home planet because life was too dull for him there. He had wanted adventure, glory, a lifetime of intense emotion. Instead he had become a soldier and found only war. He had just come off the front lines and been assigned to a training division. He was the Field First Sergeant, and they called him Sarge.

Most humans would have called Sarge a lizard—a tall, upright lizard who walked on his pair of legs more gracefully than most humans, a lizard with strangely humanlike eyes (world-weary, the look of one who's seen more than he'd expected), a lizard with a lean and muscular torso and long prehensile fingers that never stopped moving. His face, though as close to grizzled as a greenish, unevenly scaled visage could be, had a sculptured look, as if the sculptor had wanted his fingers to form a face that could simultaneously frighten children and draw respect from adults. Its most disconcerting fea-

ture for a human observer was the pair of narrow elongated
holes in the center of the face which functioned as both an
organ of breathing and an aid to speech. While his small slash
of a mouth was capable of forming words in many languages,
he could not vocalize them without the aid of vibrations from
a thin membrane just inside his long nostrils. The combined
sounds from mouth and nose could chill the coating off a
skeleton's bones. What it did to live listeners was the stuff of
nightmares.

Sarge stood in front of a large scanner console watching on
its screen Apollo confront the peasant who had taken the animal. Sitting at the scanner console was the Sarge's chief aide,
Barra. Barra was a partially humanoid being. His apparently
normal human body was topped, however, with an extraordi-
narily long thin neck leading up to a small head with heavy
lidded eyes, a long pointed nose, and heavy lipped mouth.
Although his head was small, it contained an intelligent and
clever brain, one that Sarge relied on. Barra appeared to have
what most humans would call a pot belly. Actually, since Barra
came from a desert planet, the belly was a storage organ with
several compartments, some for food, some for water. He could
live on the nutrition he stored for some time and, in fact, rarely
was seen at the company mess hall.

Both Barra and Sarge were fascinated by the disgust which
the new human being showed at the idea of eating the animal
alive. The animal had, after all, been located by a tracking
mechanism in the belt Apollo wore. In Sarge's cult there were
elaborate food rites involving both cooked and uncooked food,
but on Yevra it was considered the custom to take any food at
any time, wherever it was found and in whatever state of life
or death. An army had to be opportunistic when it came to
food. Sarge himself had been forced to violate the food customs
of his cult almost daily since he had come to Yevra.

Barra turned away from the screen after they had watched
Apollo bury the animal.

"You think he's from a vegetarian species, Sarge?" he asked.

"Maybe, but he's probably just a softhead. A being with
values. Humanoids tend to be soft when they first get here.
Especially the civilized ones. Give him time, and he'll be like
the other one, tearing at animal skin with his teeth."

"But he looks like a good prospect for us, don't you think?"

Using his neck like a fulcrum, Sarge's head made a brisk and awkward side to side movement. It was his species' version of a nod.

"I do think," Sarge said. "His musculature is impressive, and there is a keen intelligence in his eyes. Definitely a good prospect."

"Should we bag him now?"

"No, give him some time. I'd like to examine him further."

"But what if somebody from the Pelters spots him?"

"We have to take that chance. Fortunes of war. Activate the directional on his belt."

"Right, Sarge."

The stubby digits that passed for fingers on Barra's hand made some lightninglike movements on his console. On the screen it was clear that Apollo was being guided in a direction out of the forest toward a main road that passed nearby. He began to walk along the road. His steps were slow and careful in spite of the tugs from the belt. Apollo's caution impressed Sarge. He also liked the way the man appeared to be checking every potentially dangerous area. He looked like a first-rate fighter.

"Where's the other man now?" Sarge asked Barra.

"Very close."

"Bring them together."

Barra's affirmative reply sounded quite gleeful. Barra liked playing with the console, guiding the movements of new potential victims.

As Apollo passed a thick-trunked tree, a blurred shape jumped out at him. The ambush knocked Apollo off balance, but he recovered quickly and rushed his assailant. The two immediately grappled in a flurry of fists and kicking legs.

"This should prove a useful test, Corporal Barra," Sarge said. "We should see his mettle now."

Apollo quickly realized his opponent was his fighting equivalent, matching him in strength and swiftness. He had to exert all his strength to knock the ambusher to the ground. He jumped on him, intending to pin him. Then he saw the man's face for the first time.

"Croft!"

"Huh?" Croft seemed not to recognize the name at first, but

his body relaxed under Apollo's grip. "I don't—this is—Croft?"

Apollo released him. Sitting next to him, he nevertheless remained wary, ready to resume the fight.

"Croft, what's wrong?"

Croft shook his head several times, as if trying to shake a demon out of it.

"Croft. Croft is my name. That's right. And you're . . . you're Apollo. Apollo. We . . . we came here together."

He kept shaking his head. The action did seem to clear it.

"Are you sick?" Apollo asked, putting his hand on Croft's arm.

"I don't know. I couldn't, couldn't remember there for a moment. All thought went out of my head, and then I jumped you. I didn't even recognize you. I just felt you were an enemy. I'm all right now. How'd we get here, Apollo?"

"Wish I knew. I just woke up in a meadow not far from here, in these clothes."

Croft glanced down at his own garments, which were a near match of Apollo's.

"How about you?" Apollo asked him.

"I don't exactly remember. I was with you guys and suddenly I was walking along over there. My ankle was in pain and I had to sit and rest it awhile. Where's Sheba? Is she with you?"

"No. She must be nearby though. We'll seek her out. Let's try staying along this road."

The belt wanted him to take the road, he could tell that. He was curious about where the belt was leading him. He helped Croft up, and they began to walk. Croft kept shaking his head every few steps. He couldn't seem to get his mind to work right.

"Where are we?" he asked. "Any idea?"

"Presumably the planet we landed on. I feel like we've been captured but I don't know why. And by whom?"

"I don't know anything about that. But this place, for all its beauty, feels to me like the land just east of Hades."

"Know what you mean."

Apollo and Croft both shuddered involuntarily.

Sarge and Barra continued to observe Apollo and Croft on the scanner screen, whose pictures were sent back by cameras and recording equipment hidden inside the trunks of the roadside trees. They had enjoyed the meeting between Croft and Apollo very much.

"The new one is an acceptable specimen, too, I believe," Barra said.

"Agreed," Sarge replied. "This may turn out to be an unusually good catch, Barra."

"Unusually so."

"They seem so determined. We see so little determination."

Barra pointed to the screen, at Apollo pointing to his left.

"Someone over there," Apollo said. "Looks like it might be Sheba."

Croft followed the line Apollo's finger indicated. He saw a tall woman lying on the ground, her long dark brown hair seeming to stretch out in several directions.

"It is, I think," Croft said and started to run toward the supine woman. Apollo followed him closely.

Sheba's eyes were open but dazed. They had been open for some time, but she hadn't really seen anything. Now, as she sat up, she saw two men running toward her. She started scrabbling along the ground away from them. The fear in her eyes was near to panic. She had no idea what these men wanted of her, but doubted it was for anything good.

"No," she screamed. "Don't touch me! I'll kill you if you touch me, you bastards."

"Sheba," Croft said, coming to a halt a few meters from her.

She stopped going backwards and, confused, stared at this broad-shouldered man with the strange weatherbeaten face.

"She-ba?" she said. "Sheba." She realized it was her name. "How do you know me?"

Croft walked to her slowly and knelt down beside her. His eyes were uncharacteristically gentle and kind.

"It's me. Croft. And Apollo."

She studied the faces of both men. Apollo's friendly smile calmed her. Then she recognized the men.

"A-pol-lo? Yes, Apollo. And Croft. My head, it's full of images, strange things."

"Take it easy, darling," Croft said. It seemed right for him to call her darling, although she was vaguely aware he had never called her that before with such gentleness. "I was this way when I came to," he said. "Didn't know who I was or where I was."

"Where . . . are . . . we?"

He smiled. The smile, she faintly realized, was a different look for him. Croft usually only smiled at his own sarcastic remarks.

"Still working on that one, lovely," he said. "Take your time."

"I'm beginning to remember."

As Apollo and Croft had done before her, she recalled their landing on the planet, and their subsequent search of the terrain.

"Then you . . . you started to disappear, Apollo. It was like there were these wavering lines all around you. Then I passed out and woke up here. I've been just lying here, no real thoughts in my head. It was like I've been looking at this world just the way an animal does, an animal without intelligence or language." She shuddered. "It's frightening, you know?"

Croft helped her to her feet, then turned to Apollo.

"Well, Captain, what do we do now?"

"Try to find our Vipers, get the hell away from here."

"And how do you suggest we do that?"

"I don't know. I think we should take a good look around."

"Any idea of where to start?"

As soon as Croft asked the question, all three warriors felt the same gentle pull northward from their belts. In that direction, appearing to be at road's end, was an aura of light. Apollo gestured toward it.

"Well, as good a plan as any, I suppose," Croft said. "You up to a little walk, Sheba?"

Sheba, her head clearer now, smiled. She was definitely not accustomed to such politeness from Croft.

"I can make it," she said. "I hope we can find a place with some clothes more comfortable than this outfit."

"It fits you well, though. Very well."

"Now, that's more the Croft I know. I was getting worried you'd changed."

"Not me. Let's go, troops."

Led by Apollo, they started walking toward the light. Croft once looked over his shoulder, toward the trunk of a tree. Without realizing there was a camera planted there, he felt he was being watched.

• • •

At Sarge's headquarters, Croft appeared to look right at them through the screen. Barra leaned backwards, and Sarge almost took a step away from the screen. The man looked formidable. Sarge was pleased.

"I like all three of them, Sarge," Barra said. "I think we can use the lot. Shall we snare them?"

Barra's eagerness always impressed Sarge. There was nothing like new recruits to make him happy.

"Soon," Sarge said, and Barra looked even happier.

CHAPTER FOUR

Guided subtly by the electronic prods in their belts, Apollo, Croft and Sheba trudged along the road in a nearly hypnotized state. Their attention was on the beacon of light which seemed to be their destination. Sometimes the light diminished in size, so much so that they could barely see it anymore, then at other times it became a strong aura, bright and wavering slightly. Their legs were in pain from weariness but they couldn't stop themselves from continuing to go forward. Sweat poured off Croft's brow as he struggled to keep up with the torrid pace Apollo and Sheba were setting. Apollo felt as tired as Croft did but didn't care to show it. Sheba merely walked in a daze. Once in a while she went off the road a few steps. Then, shaking her head, she managed to return to the others.

"No matter how far we walk," Croft said, panting, "that light seems to be the same distance away."

"Optical illusion," Apollo said. "It's just a long walk, is all."

"A long walk, is all. Tell me another one, Captain."

Noting Croft's sarcasm, Apollo glared at him. Croft seemed

27

to thrive on sarcasm and insults, and Apollo thought it would be better to avoid bantering with him. That would really annoy him.

"It's a pretty light," Sheba said softly. Her voice sounded as dazed as her eyes looked.

"Pretty?" Croft grumbled. "It's a light, and that's all it is."

Sheba appeared not to notice Croft's comment.

"Pretty," she said.

Croft decided to leave her alone. There was something spooky about her. The lady was off her nut or something. They all walked a few more steps in silence, then suddenly Apollo stopped them with a quick gesture of his right hand.

"What is it, Apollo?" Croft said.

"Listen."

"Pretty," Sheba said.

Croft realized suddenly that they were hearing music. Faintly, but clearly. Many voices. Vigorous. The tune was energetic but melodic. Croft thought it sounded like a work song or maybe the kind of chant people sang around a campfire.

"Where's it coming from?" he said.

"Up ahead, I think," Apollo said.

"Everything's up ahead," Croft said.

"Pretty," Sheba said. "Pretty music."

"You got any idea how to shut her up?" Croft said, nodding toward Sheba. Apollo ignored Croft's question. Sheba softly began to hum along with the song. She started walking toward it. Apollo recalled a Caprican legend about a young woman in love but unable to reveal her feelings to the man she loved. Frustrated, she wandered into an unknown land, drawn there by strange music. In the meantime, the man she'd loved, realizing she'd gone, went after her, questioning everyone he met, tracing her path to the strange land. He found she had gone to a place called "the city without cares." What neither he nor she knew about that city was that, once inside its borders, each would be affected by a strange perfume that emanated from a well at the city's center. The perfume brought on forgetfulness, and eventually amnesia. By the time the two lovers met again, each had forgotten the other. Seeing something familiar in each other's face, they both smiled, then passed each other by, each going on to a different destiny than either had planned. Sheba appeared to be traveling toward just such an enchanted land.

"Sheba!" Apollo hollered after her.

She turned.

"What, Apollo?"

"We don't know who's singing. You can't just walk up to them and—"

"Can't I? Of course I can."

She walked onward briskly, with purpose. Apollo glanced at Croft, who had a look of cynical amusement. They both picked up their pace to follow her.

The singing became louder. They rounded a curve of the road and saw the glow of many fires ahead of them. It was like a small aura bordered by the distant light of the city. The firelight was, however, more intense than the shimmering city aura. Sheba suddenly began to run toward the firelight.

"Sheba, no!" Apollo hollered after her.

He ran after her. Croft reluctantly pursued both of them. Sheba took an abrupt turn off the road. Apollo and Croft came to a stop at the road's edge. They stared down at a long meadow dotted with what seemed like hundreds of campfires. Around a large central fire a large group of people gathered, singing the song the three of them had been hearing.

"I know that dialect," Croft said.

"What are they singing?" Apollo asked.

"Not sure. Something about the light of a city and the freedom it offers them."

Sheba had stopped running. She was walking confidently toward the firelight. Apollo and Croft ran toward her. Suddenly two brawny men sprang from behind a massive rock and grabbed Sheba. Apollo made a ghost move toward where his lasergun holster had been, then realized he was now weaponless. Sheba squirmed in the arms of the man who had seized her. Apollo and Croft charged at the two attackers. Before he had even landed a blow, Apollo noticed that both wore the same kind of belt he, Croft and Sheba had come awake wearing.

Other men appeared from other hiding places. Apollo punched one attacker in the face just before another of the ambushers had flung him to the ground. Looking up, he saw Croft reeling from a blow to his stomach. Apollo got to his feet and threw a solid left hook to the ugly bearded face of one of the men, but two more jumped him and pinned him against a rock. Croft was knocked to the ground and held there by another pair of men.

One of the ambushers, a thick-muscled tall man with a scrawny beard, walked up to Apollo, smiled at him, displaying several broken teeth, and said:

"Welcome to the caravan, friends. We are the friendship committee."

CHAPTER FIVE

Apollo hadn't realized how hungry he'd been. The episode with the small animal had sickened him so much he'd been able to ignore all thoughts of food. Now, with a virtual feast in front of him, he found himself wanting to tear into it like a wild beast. Croft and Sheba seemed equally eager to shovel in food.

Especially satisfying and tasteful was a speckled green and red fruit which had a sweet, pulpy flavor: a kind of thin sliced yellow meat seemed tasteless after a quick jolt of spicy flavor on first bite. The wine served with the meal was too sweet, but all three of them drank it like water anyway. In plates at the side of their main dish, there was a strange deep-brown paste whose musky odors led them to taste only out of politeness.

While they consumed their meal, a small group of people watched them steadily. It was disconcerting to have so many eyes upon them, but they were too hungry to be self-conscious about their eating habits. Other species, apparently from the insect and reptile worlds, tended to stay their distance.

"I could eat this fruit forever," Sheba said, leaning back from the table. "Exquisite. Reminds me of a dish . . ." A look of sadness came over her face.

"What is it, Sheba?" Apollo asked.

"Oh, nothing. Just my . . . my father. He wasn't much around a kitchen or galley but every once in a while he got a notion to make us a meal. There was a kind of baked fruit dish, lots of different kinds of fruit on a flaky crust—God, I wish I could have that dish again!"

"Maybe you will."

"Do you think so? Do you think we'll find him again?"

"I'm sure of it."

Sheba smiled. Apollo wished he was really so sure. Sheba's father, the legendary Commander Cain, had disappeared with his ship, the *Pegasus*, during a battle with a Cylon base-star. Since Cain had always seemed so superhuman, there was already a fleet legend that he would return in a magical iridescent ship and lead the ragtag group of ships to the fabled planet Earth.

Croft, wiping the back of his hand across his mouth and moving his plate away from him, surveyed his surroundings, then leaned over to Apollo and whispered, "We gonna stay with this motley crew?"

"For the time being. They say they're going to the city, where the light is. Might as well tag along."

Seeing that the three warriors were done eating, one of the muscle-bound hairy men who had welcomed them to the camp with such force separated from his group and approached the table.

"Greetings, newcomers," the man said jovially. "Name's Beskaroon. Come from so far away from here, never even mention it. How about you folks?"

"Not far," Apollo replied guardedly. "A place just beyond the horizon."

"You say so. Never been beyond that particular horizon. Woke up someplace in that direction. Crash-landed with a good bunch of these bozos behind me. Were a starship crew. Once. Now don't know what we are. Nomads. Followers of the dust motes. A tough world here, friend."

"Then you're not natives here either?"

"Just traders gone off course. Been here, oh, about nine or

ten of this planet's days. Hate it, all of us. Place is no better than an insect's nose hairs, you ask me."

Whether he expressed an insult or resentment, Beskaroon's voice remained cheerful. There was, in his eyes, a mistrust that didn't agree with the voice's amiable cadences.

"Why do you think we're all here?" Apollo asked. "I mean, it's like we've been brought here, isn't it?"

"Agree, friend. Not a prayer of an idea, though. We been wandering around here for days. In a circle, I think. Found this caravan. Stayed. Everybody here, in same boat. Nobody knows why. You know why?"

"No."

"Welcome to the boat, friend. Might as well join us."

Apollo nodded. Beskaroon explained that the caravan was headed for the light of the city, although no one in it had ever been to the city or was certain it even existed. While they were a mixed group, there were strict rules about behavior which forbade conflicts. They were working together to reach their goal, the city of light.

Sitting at the table, taking some of the untouched food, Beskaroon reminisced about his travels as a star-trader. He wanted to get away from this planet, take his ship back to the starlanes, he said.

"Beskaroon," Apollo asked, "in your travels, places you've traded at, have you ever heard of a planet called Earth?"

Beskaroon's smile widened. He addressed his first comment back to his comrades.

"Fellas, another Earth hawk! Apollo, what to tell you? Heard about Earth all my trading days. Never got near it. A wonder of a place, heard tell. Never thought it was real myself. You?"

"Oh, it's real all right. I know it. We're headed there. We'll find it."

Beskaroon laughed heartily.

"Not if you travel this road, you won't!"

Croft noted that Apollo sounded like Commander Adama as he vowed, "We'll get away."

"What we all say," the still-laughing Beskaroon said. He stuck out his hand to shake. Apollo took it. "Together then, Captain Apollo. Me and my gang, follow you out."

"Count on it."

"Count on it."

As Beskaroon walked away from the table, Croft muttered, "Sure. Count on it. One, two, three, and we materialize in front of our Vipers, then off to the *Galactica*. I can hardly wait."

"Confidence, Croft," Sheba said. "We can do it. We've always done it before."

"Always done it before. You could put that line on gravestones across the universe."

Sheba smiled.

"Oh, you're such a cynic, Croft."

"You better believe it. Proud of it, too."

"That's part of your charm."

"Oh, then you do think I have charm, lovely?"

"I lied. Back off, Croft."

Croft smiled crookedly. He enjoyed flirting with Sheba. He thought she was a lovely woman, and was fascinated by the wide-eyed look with which she went through life. But Sheba wouldn't give him a tumble. It seemed his lot now to be a loner, a destiny he had not chosen for himself. Since the death of his wife Leda during the ice-planet mission, he had not been comfortable around women. Hell, he hadn't even been comfortable around Leda those last days. She had been his enemy and stood up against him.

Sheba was a lost cause, anyway. Clearly those wide eyes were meant for Apollo, who generally ignored her. Sheba pined, and Apollo paid no attention. Life was like that, Croft thought. Hard to get the person you want, hard to get the person you want to want you.

Beskaroon returned and spoke to Apollo. "Caravan's about to move. You folks ready? Okay then. Fall in wherever you like."

Apollo was impressed by the spectacle of the travelers assembling their gear, putting out their campfires and heading for the road. He had never before seen so many representatives of different species all in one area, all working together. When the meadow had been abandoned, there were few traces—a wisp from burning ash, large areas of flattened grass—that so many beings had just camped there.

Once the caravan was moving, a strange silence settled upon it. The attention of everyone in the caravan was focused on the light of the city. Apollo noted that the belt seemed to be giving him little tugs whenever he turned away from the light.

Apollo wondered how so many differing individuals could have wound up on this godforsaken planet. Beskaroon had said his group had landed here by accident. Were all these groups here by accident? Crash-landings and patrols? The presence of his patrol and the other groups on this planet might not be the result of accident. They seemed to have been chosen. But by whom? For what?

He told Croft and Sheba to stay alert. They looked at him with understanding but there seemed a lack of eagerness in their eyes. As the day wore on, they all fell quite naturally and almost unconsciously into the caravan's walking rhythms.

CHAPTER SIX

A few groups sang as they walked along. Some of the music was melodic, even stirring. Some of it was grotesque. Occasionally one group would compete with another for loudness and vigor. The musical results, Apollo noticed, were not especially pleasing to the ear.

Eventually, however, Apollo and his companions found themselves trudging along in a nearly mindless state. He tried to shake the numbness out of his brain by studying the countryside through which they passed. The land beside the road was overgrown with grass so green it looked more like cloth than vegetation. Beyond the grassy fields, clumps of trees growing close together were the vanguards for apparently dense forests beyond. The bark of the trees was the color of rich soil and their leaves, on branches that swept upward, had definite maroon patches among the bright green. After a few meters of traveling, the roadside landscape showed little variation, and Apollo was in a dreamlike state when he thought he heard a scream in the distance. He turned to Croft and said, "What was that?"

"What? I didn't hear anything."

The scream came again, faint and mournful.

"Didn't you hear anything that time?"

"I can't hear anything but this lousy song those alligators in front of us are vocalizing."

The next scream was louder, filled with pain. Pushing past a pair of insectoid beings, Apollo ran off the road. Immediately, his belt seemed to push at his stomach, trying to guide him back to the road. He resisted the pull and kept on running, heading for the nearest clump of trees. There had seemed to be some movement there.

"Apollo!" Croft called after him. "You're supposed to stay with the caravan."

"I'll be right back," Apollo hollered over his shoulder.

Croft shrugged and raised his eyebrows at Sheba, then the two of them ran after Apollo, who was already disappearing into the clump of trees.

For a moment he felt disoriented. His mind swam in a kind of vertigo as the belt urged him out of the forest and his mind prodded him forward toward the sound of furious activity ahead.

Once past the first line of trees, he realized the forest was darker than he'd expected. There was an unpleasantly musty smell that appeared to come right out of the middle of the trees themselves. The sound of a rustle above him made him look up. Crouching on a branch, staring down at him, was a rather fierce-looking animal whose pointed fangs stuck out from between its closed lips. It had elongated diamondlike eyes and the hair of its body was as pointed as needles. A button on Apollo's belt flashed. Without knowing how he knew, he felt the button was telling him that this animal wasn't edible. Apollo didn't mind that, so long as it wasn't carnivorous. For the moment, all it did was stare down at him and rattle its branch in a slow side-to-side motion.

Ahead of him he heard the scream again. He had to go under the animal's branch to go toward the sound. He felt a chill go through him as the branch above him rustled, but he passed under it without incident.

He came to a wide dark clearing. Very little light was getting through the overhanging branches of tall trees.

A woman in the center of the clearing was surrounded by several dark-clothed figures. They circled her in a threatening manner, taunting her in whispers. Occasionally one of them flicked a whip in her direction, and she jumped away from its snapping lash.

Apollo couldn't see the woman clearly, although she was in better light than anyone else. She was slim and apparently tall. She was dressed in a long flowing gown whose color was difficult to distinguish in the clearing's dimness. He could see that she had long dark hair, probably black, which whirled outward at even the small movements of her head. He could not see her face. She held her hands in front of it.

Some words of the mob rose above the sinister whispering.

"We warned you, strumpet."

"Your death shan't be on our souls, woman."

"We won't have to look at your ugly face again."

"Ugly, ugly."

"Her face is the sign of evil."

"We have to eradicate evil."

"Kill her. Kill her now!"

The mob began to close in on the woman. Turning, she tried to run away, but others blocked her way. There was no way she could go, and she sank to the ground.

Apollo didn't know what cultural rite he might be interfering with, but he didn't care. Whenever you got a mob threatening an individual, that individual needed help. He rushed forward, right into the mob, flinging people aside as he swept into the central area, where the woman was curled up on the ground, her face covered with her dark hair. He stood over her and turned toward the obvious leaders of the mob, shouting, "Stand back. We're going out of here."

A man, whose muscles were no doubt as thick as his head, stepped forward. The eyes of the man, which Apollo could see in the dim light, were cruel.

"Out of the way, meddler," the man said. "This is our business."

"Killing's the business of the mob, eh?" Apollo said, his eyes darting from face to face, perceiving that everyone's eyes had the same cruel look in them. "Business as usual? Not this time, big fellow. Don't try anything."

The man laughed scornfully.

"Why, you're just a shrimp."

He jumped at Apollo who, sidestepping, landed a solid

punch on the right side of the man's face. The man collapsed, unconscious. Two other muscular representatives of the mob sprang at Apollo. Throwing punches furiously, he decked both of them. Leaning down, he grabbed the woman and, again without looking at her, made her stand up. Whispering to her to run, he pushed her forward. They both sped through the wide-eyed crowd, most of whom were apparently too stunned by the sudden move to interfere.

"After them!" someone behind him shouted. "Don't let them go."

Hearing the frantic sounds of pursuit behind him, Apollo raced after the woman through the forest. As the sounds of the crowd faded, Apollo heard sounds above them, as if the strange kind of tree-dwelling animal he'd seen earlier was tracking them. He didn't look up to check.

Suddenly there were two figures next to Apollo, both of them running, too. He tensed, ready to fight off more members of the mob, then he saw it was Croft and Sheba.

"Are we running for a reason?" Croft shouted. Apollo didn't answer.

"You need the exercise, Croft," Sheba said. "For your flab."

"My flab does just fine without exercise."

There was light ahead. The woman ran to it. Apollo and the others followed. They all came out into a section of the brightly landscaped field. The woman fell to the ground, and Apollo collapsed beside her. Croft and Sheba stood over them.

"Okay, now you can tell me," Croft said. "What was that all about?"

Catching his breath, Apollo explained what had happened. As he talked, he stared at the back of the woman's head, wanting her to turn and look at him.

"But why were they going to kill her?" Sheba said.

"They were afraid of me," the woman said, without turning. Her voice was deep, and a little husky. "Everyone is afraid of me. You should have let them kill me."

"Have you done something wrong?" Apollo asked.

"No. Not here. Not among them. They think I cast spells."

"Why would they think that?" Sheba asked.

"Because of the spell on me. Look!"

She turned toward them. For a brief moment, Apollo thought he saw a quite lovely face—clear-skinned, bright-eyed, high-cheekboned, radiant. But instantly a shell seemed to form over that face and replace it with another. And the other was not easy to look at. It was an ugly face, with scars all over it, and lumps, and rough skin, and a few hairs growing in patches on her cheeks. Her eyes seemed enclosed by puffy skin. She had no eyebrows and her nose and mouth appeared to have no definite form. The nose was a growth and the mouth an uneven slash. There was a look of decay about her.

Apollo and the others recoiled physically at the sight of the woman. Croft thought he had seen this face in a childhood nightmare. The woman laughed hollowly, seeing their reactions.

"See?" she said. "Are you sorry you rescued me, hero?"

"N—no. Not at all. You—you—"

"Go ahead. Stutter. I affect people that way. I guess I should thank you, hero, before bidding you good-bye."

She stood up, ready to walk away.

"Wait," Apollo said, standing and looking steadily at her. "Don't go. What is your name?"

She seemed surprised he would even ask the question.

"Xiomara," she said. "A lovely name, yes? To go with my face. Don't worry. I shan't stay around you."

She took a couple of steps toward the road, saw the caravan further on, switched direction.

"Don't let her go, Apollo," Sheba said.

"Yes, Xiomara," he said. "Stay. Travel with us. We're with the caravan there."

He gestured toward the caravan, and Xiomara looked in that direction. Her twisted face twisted into a look of derision.

"You'll have to defend me there, too, hero."

"I will, I promise."

She stared at him. He could, he thought, almost see her eyes. Beneath that prison of puffy skin two beautiful eyes shimmered like ghosts. He could not quite focus on them, but they seemed to be the eyes he thought he had glimpsed before the shell of the ugly face had hidden them. As he looked at her, he noticed that the ugliness of her face did not appear to hold steady. It wavered, like a picture out of focus. He squinted and it stayed out of focus. Was the woman real? What was it she had said about casting spells? Had she cast some sort of spell upon him? There was definitely something bizarre about

Xiomara's ugliness. It was as if the features of her face could change, that it was never quite the same face you had just seen, that it changed easily like a face glimpsed in disturbed water. It seemed unreal, and sent a shudder through him.

"Promise?" Xiomara asked. Apollo nodded. "Be careful, hero. In my culture, promise carries a lot of responsibility."

"In mine, also."

She stared at him for a long while.

"All right, hero. I'll come with you and your friends. Been a long time since anybody invited me to tag along with them. But, hero, you can forget the promise. I can take care of myself, I promise *you* that."

She held out her hand to shake. Apollo took it. Her grip was firm.

"My name is Apollo. This is Sheba. The guy scowling over there is Croft. That's his natural look, don't mind it."

Croft scowled more as he said, "We better hurry, if we're going to catch up with the caravan."

He started walking, and the others followed. Apollo stayed beside Xiomara. Examining her profile, he noted there was a softness to it, as if it wasn't sharply outlined, as if its lines merely lightened to the point of invisibility. After they had walked in silence for a while, he asked, "Did you come to this planet from elsewhere, too, Xiomara?"

"Elsewhere? No, I belong here. A native. There are few of us left, I can tell you that. We didn't realize there were other planets until the war came here. We live away from the war, most of us, those of us who haven't been 'recruited.'"

"A war? There is a war here?"

Xiomara made a choking sound that sounded weirdly sarcastic.

"Yes, somewhere," she said. "But don't ask me about it. The war is what ruined me, what gave me this face."

"I don't understand."

"Well, hero, I'm afraid there's a story to it."

"Tell it."

She looked at him, clearly trying to see whether she could trust him. Then something happened to her brow which Apollo couldn't quite discern, but it was definitely a change. She spoke softly, "All right, hero. Listen."

CHAPTER SEVEN

Xiomara's voice was low, calm, untroubled. When she reached certain later parts of her story, Apollo was amazed at her composure.

"You never asked me the name of my planet, hero. You people who travel through space in your magical ships never seem interested in our names here. Our place names, our surnames, our names for things. Yet we have learned your dialects. Many of them.

"The name for my planet is Yevra. When there was no war to devastate its beauty, it was a lovely place to live, a place of abundance, a place untouched by war. I used to wonder why you starpeople would ever want to seek new worlds once you had come to Yevra. I know better now. By your standards we are a primitive people, an unsophisticated culture with little variety. Our ways simple, our beliefs direct. Still, I would rather Yevra be restored to its former beauty than travel to any distant star.

"I was raised in a village on the other side of Yevra from

here, across a vast ocean. My country is now scarred by the war, in much the same way my face is scarred. The war has lain over my beautiful country like a blanket, stifling and smothering its beauty. It was once like the country we now travel through, but even more beautiful. Now in my country flames arise still from things that shouldn't burn anymore. All villages, all cities are gone. It will be the same way here, and all over Yevra, as the war devours our planet. When the planet's beauty is gone, I don't know where the war will go. My people are dead or scattered around the still habitable areas. Only soldiers now populate my country, soldiers in special uniforms that protect them against the murderous vapors which move across the land with the ease of a breeze off the sea.

"I came to womanhood while my country was yet untouched by the war. We heard about the war but it was still elsewhere. We were told it wasn't our concern. Most of the time we didn't think about it.

"I fell in love with a young man from my village. I had known him from my early childhood. It is often that way with us, that our mates were once our playmates.

"We asked permission of the village elders to enter the first stage of our wedded life. I'm told that, in many cultures, wedding or sealing of two individuals is for a lifetime, at least for the lifetime of one of the individuals."

Xiomara's words made Apollo think of Serina, whose lifetime had been short. Momentarily, her face seemed to float in front of Xiomara's.

"Here on Yevra there are five stages to marriage. Each stage is entered through prescribed rituals. Before we could enter our first stage, we had to be questioned by everyone in the village. I don't know whether the questioning had any real purpose or whether it was just a rite to ensure our love by our repeated protestations of it. If we vowed our love often enough, we knew within ourselves that it was true. Well, we were very much in love. His name was Trelon. He looked a bit like you, hero.

"We were very happy, Trelon and I. After the minimum time period in the first stage of marriage, we elected to continue to the second stage.

"At the second stage we had to put ourselves forward for ordeal. In our historical past the stage of ordeal had often been truer to the word. Prospective mates had to endure horrendous and grueling physical tests as proofs of their worthiness for each other. In our village more modern customs prevailed. We had ritualized the stage of ordeal into a series of events that were conducted as games. Trelon and I passed these tests easily, entered second stage, and were very, very happy. By this time we were certain we'd go through all five stages and live a long and wonderful life together. That wasn't to be, of course. Not with the war.

"We prepared ourselves for third stage, which was called mutilation. Originally mutilation was a scarring procedure that, by cutting and burning the skin of each mate, displayed for all their love, loyalty and devotion. In our more civilized time, the rite called only for a small facial scar, a quick cut of the knife, as the climax to a long and complicated series of ceremonies, which included musical performance and communal poetry.

"Trelon and I had begun the procedures for applying for our third-stage mutilation when he was 'recruited' into the war. You understand, hero, that nobody actually volunteers for the war in our society. The armies choose us. We do not even choose our side. Recruiters from one side or the other are sent out to grab the most-likely specimens among us, male and female alike, and then transport us to their training centers. When they took Trelon, I cursed that they hadn't chosen to take me with him.

"We were walking in a field outside the village, Trelon and I. We were quite happy that day, discussing our future together. I remember his skin was darker that day, as it often was after we lay together.

"We heard the recruiters coming. There is a soft buzz to the flying devices they use. We knew immediately what that sound meant. There was no one else in the field with us, so we knew we would be primary targets. Taking my hand, Trelon began to pull me with him. We ran toward a distant cave, one we'd often visited for lovemaking. I think we really knew the cave was too far away, that there was no chance for escape.

"Running with my eyes staring at the ground, hearing the buzz grow louder as they came closer, I saw first the long shadows of the recruiters. They stretched far away from me, many shadows appearing to reach toward the horizon. But these shadows quickly shortened, grew tiny. I felt the wind of their flight above me. Trelon forced us to run faster. I tried to keep up with him, but I stumbled. I lost my footing. Trelon had kept hold of my hand and he dragged me forward a short distance before falling himself.

"Hugging me, he held me tight for a moment before the recruiter swept down to take him, enveloping his waist in a snare. Trelon would not at first let go of my hand. As the recruiter started to rise, I was pulled to my feet, then a short way off the ground. The recruiter jabbed Trelon's free arm with something that numbed his body. I felt Trelon's arm go limp and his fingers release me. I fell only a short way, landed on my feet. Trelon and the recruiter sped upward, joining other recruiters, some with other people in their snares. It was probably my imagination, but I thought I felt Trelon's tears as rain. Or perhaps it was merely my own tears streaming down my face.

"I called after the recruiters, begged them to take me too. In their cold and imperious way, they didn't even acknowledge me. They all became dots in the sky, high above me, before disappearing.

"I returned to my village. Everyone there knew what had happened before I got there. They could have seen it in my face even if they hadn't seen the recruiters fly over. In their faces was the relief that it hadn't been them who had been taken.

"I could have entered wedlock with another man, but my love for Trelon was too strong. Other villagers encouraged me to forget Trelon and our life together, choose another of our sturdy males, settle down again—but I refused.

"The villagers did not approve of my decision. they began to shun me as an outcast. We are a calm and loving people, but we are afraid of those among us who do not follow the will of the village. We are afraid of those whose lives do not work out according to the accepted rituals. The only way I could ever maintain my status was to choose another husband, and begin the marriage cycle again.

"See, hero, I didn't want to live with another man after Trelon had gone. There was always the chance he could escape from the army, return to me. There were stories of people who had escaped, but there were other tales of horrible fates of those who tried to escape. Still, I waited. If Trelon did return, I wanted to be there for him, and not be married to another.

"The more I felt like an outcast, the angrier I became. Even though in my mind I understood my feelings about rituals I did not really understand my own feelings. I thought I should be forgiven for what the accidents of circumstance had done to me. But nobody forgave. No one in my close family, my tribal family, or in the village itself forgave me. I had lost my mate, I was without a mate. Even the other people who had lost mates did not forgive. They stayed in their own isolation until they found new mates or they became people with blank eyes who wandered the village like pack animals, with some function but without anybody inhabiting their bodies anymore. It was said that their souls had flown away. I didn't want to be like them, but I didn't want to mate for the sake of mating. Our rituals were too important to me, too beautiful, for me to defame them. Trelon was the only mate I wanted, the only one I'd ever wanted. I could have no other.

"I don't know what made me do what I did. I had been drifting into the kind of isolation I'd seen in others. I felt my soul about to leave me."

Xiomara did not speak for a moment. She had begun to walk a little faster, as if she wanted to reach the caravan quickly and not have to finish her tale. Apollo walked patiently beside her, wanting to comfort her, feeling a strong urge to put his arm around her. When she did speak again, her voice was flat, unemotional, uninvolved with the words she spoke.

"The war came to our village. First, there were battles all around us, fighting that went on while we cowered in our homes or hid in caves. The lovely sweet air that was like an aura around the village became acrid with the smell of expended ammunition, smoke from gunbarrels, the sharp electrical odors of thousands of killing blasts from laser weapons. The blue sky over our village became gray with smoke. We didn't see our sun for many days. Our buildings were rocked by explosions close to the village. Still, the village remained untouched until after the battle.

"The winners were the soldiers from the Sky Federation, which most call the 'Sweepers.' The other side is the 'Pelters,' or the Cave Federation. The Sweepers were the ones who had taken Trelon. They have flying devices which they sometimes use in battle as well as recruiting. The Pelters live in our caves, even though they came here from some other planet. Why they choose to live in caves, I don't know. Anyway, now they are whatever they conquer; the names don't mean much.

"The Sweepers occupied our area. Seeing many of our people among these soldiers, I started asking questions about Trelon, seeking him. Most of the soldiers were too dazed or numb to talk to me. The others were surly. Not only that, they mistook my intentions, the mean ones. As I tried to leave them after getting no answer, they'd grab me and try to make love to me. After I'd managed two or three of those escapes, my common sense and I vowed not to go anywhere near the camp of soldiers again.

"However, during my last trip to the camp, one of the other soldiers had heard me say the name Trelon. The next time he came to our village he sought me out. He said he had information about Trelon that he would tell me in secret. He took me to a grove outside the village. I should have been superstitious and never gone to that place with him; this grove was where we buried our dead.

"The soldier said his name was Burist, at least that was the part of his long name that I remember. 'I served with Trelon,' he told me. 'A fighter, Trelon, one of the best.' My eyes were filling with tears as I asked, 'But where is he now?'

"Burist tried to embrace me. Not as a lover, not right then as a lover, but as a friend. However, I'd had enough of soldier's embraces at the army camp. I pulled away from him and asked the question again. His body went slack. He looked like there was nothing substantial beneath his skin.

"'Trelon is dead, my lovely,' he said. 'I'm sorry to tell you that, and I really didn't want to, but I felt he would have wanted me to.'

"I'm afraid I started crying with such force, with such choking deathlike sobs, that it frightened Burist. He tried to say soothing words to me, tried to calm me down with gentle touches. But I couldn't stop crying. My life was over, I thought. Trelon will never return. I wanted to die. Well, you may know what it felt like. There is something in your eyes that tells me you do, hero.

"I can't really explain what happened that afternoon in the

grove of the dead. I suppose I became a child's doll as far as Burist was concerned, or I was dead in his eyes and he felt some kind of necrophiliac desire for me. I don't even remember it happening. I was in a daze one moment, unable to stop crying, and by the next moment the lovemaking between Burist and me had ended. There is nothing in between that I can remember.

"After, Burist hugged me tightly and whispered in my ear how Trelon had died, how he had been brave in battle, killing scores of the enemy, then had finally met his death in a fierce battle with a giant. I doubted the giant, but I believed Trelon was dead. Burist offered to become my protector, if I would accompany him when his battalion left the camp.

"Even now I cannot find a way to show you completely how vile a being this Burist was. How vile he *is*, if he hasn't yet achieved the terrible death I have wished upon him. Screaming, I jumped at him and began clawing at his eyes. He was too strong for me, and he flung me away roughly. His face suddenly twisted in a bizarre smile, and I could see he intended to use me again. I scrambled to my feet and ran out of the grove. I heard his laughter behind me, but he did not follow. I suppose he felt there would be another time. He did not understand our ways.

"I ran a short distance in the protective darkness of trees when suddenly my path was blocked by a trio of citizens from my village. I didn't even have to question them. I saw in their eyes that they'd been spying on me and Burist in the grove of the dead. And I knew my fate was sealed. I collapsed at their feet and remember little of the next days.

"You must understand, hero, that our village regards all of the soldiers from both sides as our enemies. It doesn't matter what side invades our tranquility and steals our best individuals. They camp outside our villages and destroy our farmland for at least a season. They taunt us, and frequently kidnap us for their amusement.

"If the villagers who testified against me had seen me resist Burist, which I would have done if my mind had not been gripped by my grief, I would merely have been reprimanded and become an outcast for a short term. Since I was already a virtual outcast, that would not have been a difficult punishment for me.

"But in their eyes I had committed a crime and we punish crimes severely.

"And so they gave me this face."

Xiomara paused, turning her disfigured face toward Apollo for a full view. He managed not to grimace.

"They did that to you?" he said. "Punished you by disfiguring your face?"

Xiomara chuckled bitterly.

"Not in the way you think. It may seem odd to you, hero, but I am still beautiful. You are just unable to see it."

"I don't understand."

"You know what, hero? I adore *your* face. It has such kindness in it. Your eyes would never judge me the way my fellow villagers did. You would have forgiven me."

"I suppose I would."

"I wish you could see my face. This is the first time in ages that I even wanted someone to see my face, the first time I've even regretted the punishment the judges gave me. At the time I thought it was appropriate, and even just. And properly ironic."

They walked along a few more steps quietly. Apollo wanted to ask her questions, to clear up the mysteries she had provided, but he waited for her to tell him in her calm voice.

"If you could have seen my village, hero, before it was finally destroyed, you would not have suspected us of being anything more than a primitive people. We lived in primitive fashion—grew our own food, lived in simple lodgings, devoted our lives to the development of crafts, played the games of the ancients. But we did have some leftover technology from a more civilized and scientific time, a time before the war had somewhat simplified our existence.

"I didn't understand it all then. Then it was all magic rites kept secret by the cult of the privileged. Now, since I've fled the village and seen more of what the world has to offer, I know it's not magic.

"The magicians were our doctors, scientifically trained. They treated and cured us, but they also punished us. They could even kill us, if the law ordered. It was the custom.

"After my brief trial, during which I said not a single word, I was taken outside the village to a large dark building. All of the villagers followed me and taunted me. Even though they shouted, I could barely hear them. My own sobs drowned them out. The doctors wore ancient outfits, long black robes with black fur collars and more black fur around the hems. They wore long deep strings of red and green beads which swayed around their bodies as they walked. Their faces were hidden by masks that were twice the height and width of their heads. The masks were ugly, lumps of materials representing flesh, budlike eyes planted among the mounds of skin, more of the black fur, representing hair, packed tightly around the whole outline, a slash to stand for a mouth. They were, I suppose, faces like mine, at least as mine has been described to me. I don't see this face, you see. When I look into a mirror or a pool of water, I see my old face. My former face was beautiful, hero."

"Yes, I know," Apollo said softly. She stopped walking, stared at him. He could almost see her eyes through the lumps of puffy skin.

"How can you know?" she said, her voice rising. It was the only time emotion had come into her voice.

"I think I saw your real face once back there."

"Others have described the sensation of seeing my real face. It is strange. I can't quite picture it.

"At any rate, I was taken into the dark building and brought to a wide central fire. Its flames shot up toward the ceiling of a huge cavernlike chamber. The specially treated doctors' masks sent off many blinding rays of firelight. The doctors began to dance around the fire, their masks a dazzling and mysterious array of flickering light.

"Then I was roughly placed on a platform attached to cables which had dropped from the ceiling. My captors tied me down. The platform was raised and maneuvered to a position just above the flames. I felt the flames licking near me, coming close to my skin. The surfaces of the platform began to heat up, becoming painfully unbearable.

"Doctors in their shimmering masks floated all around me, circling the platform. How they were there, I don't know. One doctor raised his arm. In his hand he gripped an odd-shaped brazier. Vapors came out of vents in its side and drifted down toward me. I nearly fainted from fear of the vapors, and then they forced me into unconsciousness anyway.

"At the time I had no idea what had been done to me. All I knew is that I woke up alone in the big dark room. The people, villagers and doctors alike, were gone. The fire was out. The room was cold and it echoed with sound that seemed to have no source.

"I came out of the building and saw a crowd waiting for me. There were looks of shock and horror on all faces. They were, of course, staring at this grotesque and ugly visage which the doctors had so skillfully given me. Instinctively, I put my hands to my face and felt it all over. Its contours seemed no different from what I'd known before. I rushed past the horrified and sickened villagers and somehow managed to find my way to my quarters. There I took out a mirror and stared at the face I'd always known.

"It was a long while before I realized that I was the only one who ever saw that face now.

"The doctors, as I found out later, used ancient surgical techniques to implant a transmitter within me. Some say it is a little box, others that it is a set of wires, planted in my brain, which go to transmitters near the surface of my skin; others say that it is just one small microscopic bit placed somewhere beneath the skin of my face. Whatever their technology, the doctors managed to superimpose this ugly face over my real face for the rest of you to see. It is the mask which cannot be separated from me. I cannot suddenly remove it, as the doctors could remove theirs, and reveal my beauty underneath. In the time since, the face beneath the mask has become more beautiful, or certainly stronger. My eyes are more pronounced, my skin more lustrous, my lips fuller, my—well, it doesn't matter what improvements nature has given my real face. No one but me will ever see it again.

"At the time I realized the horror of the mask, I could not bear to stay in the village. Even though I had grown up there and had never been more than a short distance from it, I knew I had to flee. As I ran, I thought I heard a few voices behind me saying good riddance. I've traveled much since that time and have continually had to see the horror reflected in the eyes of people staring at me. I have had to fight off attack. I have had to escape killing. I have sometimes even had to fend off men with twisted minds who wanted to do to me what Burist had done.

"I tried to return to my village once, but it is gone, destroyed, apparently by another of the war's battles. At any rate, it is rubble. And the people of the village have disappeared. In all my wanderings, I've never encountered one of them."

Xiomara stopped speaking, and Apollo could not for a while find words to fill in the long pause that followed her tale. Finally, he said, "Isn't there anybody anywhere who can help? Any medical men who can reverse the process or remove what the doctors implanted in you?"

Xiomara laughed bitterly.

"The doctors are gone, too, with the village. If they are dead, their techniques died with them. It is said that only one of the doctors can undo the damage. Anyone else tries, and I will die. They say that, anyway. There is nothing I can do."

"Don't say that. There must be something."

In spite of the ugliness of her mouth, the smile that it twisted into seemed soft, almost pleased.

"You are extraordinarly compassionate, hero. But, no, there is nothing."

They had, by this time, caught up with the rear ranks of the caravan. Apollo noted several looks of revulsion directed Xiomara's way. She must have seen them, too. The hatred in them alerted Apollo. He knew that it would be necessary to be watchful to protect Xiomara from that hatred.

CHAPTER EIGHT

Sarge had watched Apollo's rescue of Xiomara with great interest. Gallantry was unknown in his culture. Helping strangers would have been a phenomenon leading to the commitment of the rescuer for psychiatric observation. Among Sarge's people, an individual protected his family, friends and fellow warriors without question and without a thought of the heroism that might be involved. But many of the humans Sarge had studied seemed willing to put themselves in danger to help others whom they had never seen before. Such recklessness made them good soldiers in the war, although they tended not to survive for long.

Sarge and Barra had arranged for Xiomara to be attacked by the mob in order to see if the new humans would in any way respond to it. With amplifiers placed in the trees, they had increased the volume of Xiomara's screams so that the newcomers would hear them. Sarge had been impressed with the quickness of Apollo's reaction, and the skill with which he had fought when outnumbered.

"An impressive battler, Sarge," Barra commented.

"Very impressive, Barra. The others seemed quick to react and ready to fight, too."

"I think all three of them would fight well for our side."

"Well, there is a look of stubbornness about them, I think. I can still not read a humanoid face well. They're obviously skilled at warfare. I think it's time to recruit them."

The news cheered Barra. He had a look of intense happiness on his face, although Sarge did not perceive it. He could not read Barra's face well, either. The faces of his own culture did not change with emotion, and so he had little skill in reading the faces of others.

"Yes sir, Sarge! What about the woman they saved?"

Sarge pressed a button on Barra's console and examined a close-up image of Xiomara. He did not see that she was ugly according to human perceptions, although he could tell that her somewhat lumpy face differed from the smooth and relatively uncluttered faces of her three new friends. He would not have understood the strange feelings that Xiomara caused in others.

"She looks sturdy," he said. "Take her, too. Send out the orders to the recruiters. I have to return to training now. We have a group ready to send to the front lines. Just cannon fodder, most of them, but they'll help to hold the line."

"Right, Sarge!"

Barra began, happily, to transmit the order to the recruiters.

Apollo did not know what to say to Xiomara. He had never before met anyone who had to live a tragedy day by day. At the same time he was unnerved that he could not quite focus on her face. Sometimes he saw it as the doctors had transformed it, but there were several quick flashes of what seemed to be her real face that he didn't see for long enough to hold it in his memory. Before he could narrow his eyes to look better, the mask-face had returned.

His concentration on Xiomara's face had made him forget about the hateful stares of the others in the caravan. Croft, however, felt their uneasiness growing, and he was not surprised when Beskaroon separated from his cohorts and approached him, a broad smile on his genial face.

"Your friend there keeps some strange company, don't he?" Beskaroon said, with a nod toward Apollo. Croft glanced back, and he smiled cynically.

"No worse than the company I keep, I guess," he said.

At first Beskaroon did not perceive that Croft's insult was directed at him, then he spoke angrily, "Wouldn't cross swords with me, I were you, Croft."

Croft's face relaxed into injured innocence.

"Why'd I do that? I think you're a sweetheart, Besky."

Beskaroon, a bit flustered, waved his arms as he spoke: "Knew the two of you were trouble, minute I saw you."

Sheba, coming out of her daze, said, "Three of us."

Beskaroon swung around to face her.

"What?" he said.

"Three of us. Far as you're concerned, we're all trouble."

"Closing ranks, huh? Like all you warrior types. Don't know what's good for you, do you?"

"Nutrition," Croft said. "Nutrition's what's good for us. And a healthy attitude and the seven daily—"

"Shut up, Croft," Beskaroon growled.

Croft smiled. He was enjoying Beskaroon's bemused anger.

"You the type backs up your words, Besky?"

Beskaroon choked out his words: "Count on that, Croft."

Beskaroon and Croft squared off and began to circle around each other. Beskaroon growled incoherently. Croft's grin grew and he felt a rush of adrenaline. Fighting Beskaroon was at least something worth doing.

Apollo, seeing the two in fighting attitude, rushed forward, shouting, "What's going on?"

Croft addressed Apollo without taking his eyes off Beskaroon.

"Big guy here doesn't approve of us. He'd like to mix it up."

Beskaroon growled an agreement. Apollo stepped in front of Croft.

"Forget it, Croft. Take it easy, Beskaroon. There's no point in fighting among ourselves."

"Doesn't have to be a point," Beskaroon muttered.

"He doesn't approve of your new friend, Apollo," Croft said. "Says she's weird."

"She's ugly," Beskaroon said. "Don't like ugly here, none of us. None of us humans, anyway. Scaleskins don't even know from ugly. Makes us sick to our stomachs, her ugly face. Won't have it here."

Apollo made a sound in his throat that was not much different than the growlings Beskaroon had been making, and he lunged forward. Xiomara, who had run up, grabbed his arm and said calmly, "That's just the kind of treatment I always get, Apollo. Don't get yourself in a mess over it. Please."

The soothing quality of her voice allowed Apollo to relax. Stepping back from Beskaroon, he said, in a voice nearly as calm as Xiomara's, "If you say so. Leave us alone, Beskaroon."

Beskaroon, still grumbling, rejoined his comrades. Croft called after him, "Take it easy, Besky."

After they had walked awhile in silence, their belts gently tugging them toward the city of light, Apollo edged toward Croft and whispered, "See how they're giving us a wide berth?"

"It didn't escape my notice, Captain."

Even as they talked, several of the human travelers glanced balefully toward Xiomara. There seemed to be something brewing.

"We'll have to be careful," Apollo said.

"Maybe we should split away from these guys, get to that city on our own."

"Maybe."

Xiomara had quietly come up behind them.

"No," she said, startling both men. "Don't. Not for me. I'm used to treatment like this. I can take care of myself."

Apollo recalled the difficulty she had had taking care of herself back in the forest, but decided not to mention it to her.

"It's a funny thing," she said. "Until they gave me this face, I couldn't really take care of myself. I relied on Trelon for strength. Since the face, well, I've had to become strong. And not just phsyically. I can't tell you the insults I've had to endure, the cruel behavior. But I can handle myself."

"I'm sure you can," Apollo said, "but it's—"

"And please don't see yourself as my protector, hero, just because you got me out of one scrape. I need no protector. Anyway, you'll have enough on your hands, all three of you, just taking care of yourself. Yevra's a tough world. We all have to look out for ourselves."

"Is that right?" Apollo asked. Xiomara nodded. They walked a few steps. Apollo studied the roadside scenery, then he realized that Xiomara might feel his gaze was focused in that direction because he didn't care to look at her. He looked at her. "Okay," he said, "this may be, as you say, a tough world, and you may have your ways. But they're not mine. Not ours. We don't just look out for ourselves. We look out for our friends, our wingmates, the people in our society who need help. We look out for everybody. In my job I am responsible for the welfare of people I don't even approve of, people I don't like."

As he spoke, the faces of the diabolical Sire Uri and the weak-willed members of the *Galactica's* Council of Twelve, the dozen deadbeats as he called them, seemed to float in front of him. There had been many times when he had wanted to leave them behind on one of the planets the fleet had visited.

"That's all very nice, hero. But, as you say, it's your way. I don't need you. Any of you. I would let you die, if it meant saving myself."

"An ugly idea, Xiomara."

"Ugly people can speak ugly ideas. It's our right."

The moment he had used the word ugly, Apollo had felt a strong twinge of regret. He wanted to apologize to her, but he realized it would only compound the insult if he did, so he remained silent. A weird crooked smile came into Xiomara's face.

"Smile, Captain. You have such a serious expression all of the time. Your eyebrows bend down to meet the beginning of your nose. And your eyes, they're so . . . intense. Your lips are so grim."

"Boy, she's got you pegged, buddy," Croft commented.

Xiomara turned toward Croft.

"Why aren't *you* repelled by me?" she asked. "Are you and Apollo so much alike?"

Croft burst into mocking laughter.

"Hardly," he said. "We're from two different worlds. Literally from two different worlds. Apollo's a Caprican. They're logical and calm most of the time, but not without a fierce temper when you can bring it out. I'm from Scorpia. We Scorpians are more devious. Crafty, difficult to get along with, inclined to be cynical. My world, I guess, is a lot like yours, Xiomara."

"The way it is now. Not the way it used to be before the war came down from the skies. But I don't want to think about the war. I want to think about happy things. Music and dancing.

I used to know a dance. Let me show it to you."

Humming softly to herself, Xiomara began to dance. Starting slowly, with tiny childlike steps, she circled the two men. As her humming became louder, her dancing became more vigorous. And, Apollo noticed, more sensual in the writhings of her entire body. With the sensuality came a look of happy abandonment. Apollo wondered if it was a release of some of the frustration which she must feel. The melody she hummed had a lilt, Apollo thought, like the best of the *Galactica's* chanteys, combined with the lovely birdlike sounds of the delicate Caprican tunes he remembered from his childhood.

She raised her right leg and twirled. Looking past her, Apollo saw that other men in the caravan had stopped to watch her. But they were not a friendly audience. Beskaroon was mumbling something to his nearest comrades, and they were nodding with a conspiratorial smugness. He jabbed Croft in the shoulder, told him to look toward Beskaroon and his scurvy bunch. Sheba, who'd already seen the trouble brewing, joined Apollo and Croft.

"Yeah, I noticed," Croft said. "I think Besky's planning a move. What do you think we should do?"

"Nothing yet. Just be ready."

Xiomara, unmindful of the threats surrounding her, continued her dance, which was more frenetic now. The music coming out of her throat had become more primitive. Backing up in a series of graceful swaying moves, she shouted toward Apollo, "It's bizarre seeing something so grotesque as I become so graceful, isn't it, hero?"

Without waiting for an answer from him, she reached her arms toward the sky in a gesture that suggested supplication, and began to spin very slowly. She was now quite close to Beskaroon and his group. She appeared to be deliberately tantalizing them. She rushed toward him like a charging animal, then abruptly stopped and danced away. Beskaroon's body shook with anger. She made another charge, another retreat, and Beskaroon's face darkened. He made a brief grab after she was out of reach. Apollo, Croft and Sheba edged forward.

Gracefully she swept toward Beskaroon and his group again. With a cry of fury, Beskaroon jumped toward her. With a wide smile making her face more grotesque, Xiomara danced right out of his outstretched arms. His comrades joined him, and the group began to charge toward Xiomara. Reacting instantly, the three warriors from the *Galactica* intervened their bodies between Xiomara and the advancing horde. Croft noticed that a horde was exactly what Besky and his bunch looked like—a surging line of wild animals out to ravage everything in sight.

Apollo coolly jabbed at Beskaroon, catching him on the nose, making him yelp in pain, forcing him backward. Croft tripped up another of the attackers while Sheba decked a big man with a punch to his stomach. For a moment the others seemed stunned, with their leader and two of his allies squirming on the ground, but Beskaroon made a throaty sound that was some kind of battle cry and the men stampeded toward the Galacticans, some of them brandishing knives. Apollo found himself kicking one man, then quickly elbowing another in the face. Croft just kept punching, never sure where the blows were landing. Sheba heard bones snap as she drop-kicked one of Beskaroon's men in the ribs. Xiomara, with moves not much different from those in her dance, managed to deck a pair who had jumped toward her. Apollo saw another one about to hit Xiomara from behind, and he shouldered the attacker to the ground and knocked him unconscious with a blow to his head. Standing up, he saw that all his allies were in trouble. Croft caught his eye and shouted, "Let's get the hell out of here!"

Sometimes it was better to retreat from the odds, and the Galacticans, with Xiomara, began to back up. Turning suddenly, they raced off the road, feeling a slight tug from their belts, urging them to return. Some of Beskaroon's men stopped at the edge of the road. The rest, led by a yelping Beskaroon himself, continued the pursuit into the adjoining field.

Croft stumbled over a patch of twisted grass. He fell to the ground so hard that his breath was knocked out of him. Sheba helped him up. Beskaroon and his mob were now very close.

High in the sky there was a high-pitched hum. Xiomara was the first to hear it. She stopped running abruptly and stared at what looked like a clear sky above her. Apollo, running back to her, looked up. He could see nothing except what appeared to be a few birds. Glancing toward the rear, he saw Beskaroon's mob gaining on Croft and Sheba.

"They're catching up, Xiomara!" he shouted. "Run!"

"No point in it. That sound, it's them!"

"Them? Who?"

"The recruiters. It's the damn recruiters!"

She pointed upward. Apollo found out that the dots that had seemed to be birds had grown suddenly to large proportions. Squinting against the bright light in back of them, he saw they were figures in flying outfits. Thin vapor trails drifted out of packs on their backs. They were swooping downward.

"Run, Apollo," Xiomara whispered huskily. Even as he heard the panic in her voice, he realized it was the first time she had addressed him as anything other than "hero." "Get away, before they get you."

"Xiomara—"

"Run! Please, run!"

She pushed against his shoulders violently. He grabbed her hand and started to pull her along with him. She pulled out of his grasp and gestured for him to run on his own. Ahead of them, Croft and Sheba were running. Croft was looking upward over his shoulder at the recruiters. Behind them, Beskaroon had almost caught up, apparently unaware of the danger in the skies.

"No, Apollo, no!" Xiomara screamed as a recruiter descended upon him. Just before the recruiter grabbed him, Apollo looked up and saw his assailant. Twisting sideways, he seized the recruiter's legs and pulled him downward. The move caught the recruiter by surprise and Apollo was able to slam him to the ground. The hum of the creature's flying device came to an abrupt halt and the creature, a lizardlike being, went limp.

Nearby Croft was in a fierce battle with another of the recruiters, but was losing. The recruiter had one of Croft's legs already off the ground. Croft's other leg lost contact with the ground as the recruiter swept him upward. Captured, Croft nevertheless kicked wildly, making contact now only with air.

Suddenly the sky above them was dense with recruiters. Beskaroon and his mob finally saw them and immediately began scattering in all directions. They became easy prey for the recruiters, who picked them off.

Xiomara stood still in the middle of the chaos, her sad frightened eyes concentrating on Apollo. She mouthed his name silently. Apollo was snatched in a sneak attack. One recruiter drew him forward while another flew down behind him, grabbed his shoulders and lifted him like a child. Like Croft, he struggled in the recruiter's grasp. In the distance he saw Sheba in the arms of another of the creatures.

Soon only Xiomara was left on the ground. She stared up at the now retreating recruiters with their new captives, and she did not see the lone remaining creature who flew down, plucked her off the ground and made her the last recruit of the raid.

CHAPTER NINE

Numbness seeped through Apollo's body. The recruiter had jabbed his arm with something, apparently a chemical to make him go limp. The other victims appeared to hang immobile from the grasps of their recruiters.

Picking up speed, the recruiters soared higher. At this height, Apollo noticed, the air was much colder, stinging the skin of his face. He could freeze to death. His body was so numb from the chemicals, he wouldn't be able to tell. The recruiter holding Sheba flew by. Sheba's eyes were closed. She looked dead. These bastards would let her die, wouldn't they, as they indifferently carried their prey.

He lost sight of Sheba and her recruiter as they disappeared into the flying crowd. The flying horde was an impressive sight, scores of recruiters grouped tightly together and flying in a loose but definite formation. In one pass, he saw Beskaroon still fighting the chemicals and struggling in his recruiter's hold. There seemed no point in struggling though. One of the lessons he'd learned back in space academy was that a warrior, once he knows he's captured, shouldn't fight back futilely but use his energy to look for escape opportunities. Beskaroon's struggle at this height was absurd, anyway. If he did break the recruiter's hold, it was a long fall to the ground.

Nothing to do now but see where these louses were taking their prizes. Since Xiomara had said the recruiters captured soldiers for a war, the chances were their destination was a military one. He was eager to get there. Then he could find the way out.

A cloud of doubt crossed Apollo's mind. *What am I thinking of?* he thought. *I go along assuming we're going to escape. We've been in scrapes before and we've always escaped. How can I believe that now? We're stranded on a planet. We don't know where our ships are. We don't know where any ships are. We may never see the* Galactica *again.*

Apollo remembered the prophecy. He didn't know where the story had come from, but it had swept the ship. Suddenly everyone knew it had been predicted that most of the people aboard the *Galactica* would not reach Earth. The prophecy went on to state that perhaps Earth would not be reached by the people in the present fleet but by other generations. Commander Adama and his command staff had done their best to quell the rumor, but it still remained, whispered in dark corridors, printed in privately circulated pamphlets. There were always dissidents ready to pounce on any piece of information or speculation that would cause doubts throughout the easily swayed population of the ragtag fleet.

Although he put no store in idle rumors, Apollo couldn't help wondering now if the prophecy in some way applied to him. It was beginning to look like he was one of the people who wouldn't reach Earth. There had been times when Apollo had regarded the quest as his father's folly, a simple goal that had grown into an obsession. He had sometimes criticized his father for putting too much energy into the quest, and his father replied that faith was always worth an excess of energy. Now, stuck on this lousy planet, literally in the clutches of an enemy, Apollo couldn't bear the thought of not seeing if the quest had an end, nor did he particularly relish spending the remainder of his days on this planet.

His recruiter took an abrupt turn and Apollo suddenly saw, looming in front of him, an enormous ship gliding across the sky toward them. It was an odd-looking ship, awkwardly con-

structed and looking as if it were assembled with spare parts
and then painted all over in a dismal gray. Its surfaces were
plain, with nothing ornate visible, not even an insignia. He
couldn't recall any ship with this superstructure design in any
warbook he'd studied, and that included every warbook he'd
memorized since he'd first entered the academy.

As the recruiters headed toward the ship, a large segment
of it came open. The opening looked to Apollo like a large
mouth about to attack and chew up the recruiters and their
captives. The recruiters picked up speed and, with no transition
from light to darkness, he and his recruiter were suddenly inside
the ship and enveloped in what seemed like total blackness.

He felt himself being carried along through frigid air, pen-
etrating the darkness further. He could see nothing. He heard
only the sound of flight around him, felt only the dank cold of
the breeze against his skin. Suddenly, Beskaroon uttered an
expletive. He sounded as if he were right behind Apollo. Others
reacted to the sound, and there were some moans, some shouted
words.

He had a sense of being lowered, and his still slightly numbed
feet were soon dragging against a soft padded floor. He felt
the recruiter gently release him and he stumbled forward in the
pitch black. He heard the soft plops of others being deposited
all around him. A moment passed before he realized that the
floor was moving him forward. He guessed it was a belt carrying them all further into the ship's interior. Concentrating on
keeping his balance, he took a couple of necessary steps sideways and bumped into another individual.

"Who is it?" the person said. Apollo recognized Croft's
voice.

"Croft!"

"Apollo! Is that you?"

"Yes."

"Where are we?"

"I don't know. Inside a ship. On a moving belt of some
sort. Can't tell you anything more than that."

"What's happening, do you think?"

"Don't know that either. We're either being taken somewhere or—"

"Or what? Being disposed of, you mean?"

"Maybe. But I doubt it. Too much trouble in transporting
us here. Xiomara said they were recruiters."

"Recruiters?"

"They grab off people to put them in an army. Kind of a forced draft or conscription. We'll just have to—"

Apollo stopped talking because they abruptly felt themselves passing through a series of cloth strips. As the last of the cloth strips brushed past his face, Apollo's eyes were stung by the bright light in a new room. He squinted and gradually brought the world around him into focus. First he saw what he recognized as a control panel, even though he'd never before seen one with such bizarre configurations. On it were many strange symbols, all of which looked like miniature paintings. He had never seen picture writing so intricate. There must have been a mountain of information within each fancily designed pictograph. There were no levers, buttons or touchplates anywhere on the panel. Instead, there were many small black and green rectangles, each of which had a different number of tiny holes on its surface.

He felt new movement next to him and, taking his attention away from the control panel, he found himself looking up at what appeared to be a giant. Even when he brought the being into focus, it still looked like some kind of mythological monster. A reptilian monster in military garb. Thin arms emerged from short sleeves. The surface of the arms, and that part of the creature's legs that Apollo could see, were spiny and slightly hairy. The spines themselves were sharp, colored a dark pink, and relatively hairless. Long curly hairs were scattered around the base of each spine. The spines themselves went in riverlike lines to the creature's hands. The hands were four-fingered, with each finger ending in sharp points without any sign of fingernails. There were a couple of tiny spines where the joint should have been on the being's largest finger, which was located on the sides of his hands.

Apollo looked higher, into the face of the creature. It was the face of a lizard, with more spines along its side, which looked like pointed sideburns. Some hair was scattered over the cranium of the creature's head and on his high cheekbones, which jutted out far. The creature's eyes, hidden by the cheekbone ridge, were difficult to see. It had only holes for a nose, and a twisted slash of a mouth. Its massive shoulders duplicated the jut of his cheekbones, seeming to stretch beyond the normal lines of his torso.

When the creature spoke, its words were understandable but

distorted. There were secondary sounds that Apollo quickly saw were caused by the vibrations of the being's nose holes.

"Get up scum," the creature said.

"Who are you?" Apollo said. "Why are—"

"Shut up, stupid. Do what you're told, all of you. Get up!"

No one made a move, and Croft muttered, "Take a hike, flybrain."

The creature switched his attention to Croft and said in an angry voice: "Oh, you're the tough one in the group, is that right, boy?"

"Tough enough to—"

Before Croft had a chance to finish his sentence, the creature lifted him up and held him away from his body, then he flung Croft with incredible force against a nearby wall. Croft's eyes went blank as soon as he hit the wall and he slid to the floor, unconscious.

"All right," the creature barked, "the rest of you scum, stand up and stand straight. *Now!*"

Most of the captives did stand up, but a trio was left sitting defiantly on the floor. Apollo, Sheba and Xiomara. Gesturing with his head toward a subordinate, the creature ordered the standing group to line up against the wall where Croft sat shaking his head from side to side. Then it walked to Apollo and stood over him.

"A classic case, eh?" it said. "I get at least one of you every batch. I thought you were the type the first I saw you, when you stood up to that filthy flesh-eater. Later, too, when you fought the—"

"You've been watching me all this time?"

"You and your friends, yes. You're a tough bird, and our army always needs a few tough birds."

"Army? You think we'll fight for your—"

"You'll find you'll have little choice." The creature's voice had become smoother. "Here on Yevra anyone we choose fights for us. Unless the other side grabs them first. I know you scum come from elsewhere. One of our officers saw you land, brought you through the camouflage force field to us."

Apollo raised his hand.

"Wait," he said. "You're going too fast for me. You snatched us for your army?"

"That is correct. We're always on the lookout for new vermin, and you people just flew into our laps, you might say."

"And about the force field—camouflage?"

"Some intruders from elsewhere have tried to interfere with our little war here, have tried to bring peace. Negotiations. Talks. We took care of them, but we want no more of that kind of intruder. The force field hides us from outside observation. Anyone investigating Yevra sees a barren planet, instead of the rich and fruitful place it is. Only a few of the dismally curious manage to find their way here. Like you folks."

"We're willing to leave," Sheba said.

The creature turned toward her, and its voice dropped to a mean whisper.

"You'll need your vehicles, won't you? You see, we have them, too."

Apollo stood up, stared defiantly at the creature.

"I'm Captain Apollo from the *Battlestar Galactica*. I demand you return our vipercrafts to us and give us free passage away from—"

The creature moved threateningly toward Apollo.

"Don't even bother making heroic plays, scum. You're suggesting that your puny battlestar can avenge you. They can't even find you."

"Don't be too sure of that."

"All right, we'll be cautious. But we're not worried. Now, vermin, since you're such a fine leader, assemble these troops into an orderly line."

"No." Apollo's voice was even quieter than the creature's.

"Apollo," Sheba whispered, "you saw what he did to Croft."

"Yep. He's gonna have to do it to me, too."

"My pleasure, scum."

The creature tried to lift Apollo up with the same motion he'd used on Croft. However, Apollo was prepared for the attack and he broke out of the hold easily, in spite of the creature's immense strength. While the creature stood still, surprised by the human's retaliation, Apollo barreled into its midsection, ramming it with his elbow. He must have found a weak spot, for the creature doubled over, holding on to the area. The creature reeled backward. A pair of its aides rushed forward, but the creature waved them away, saying in a slightly out-of-breath whisper, "No, scum like this need a lesson."

"And I'm sure you're ready to be the teacher," Apollo said.

The creature charged at Apollo like a wild beast. Apollo, who had had abundant practice in this kind of frontal assault, dodged sideways easily while managing to land a firm punch on the side of the creature's face. He felt some crunch and give as the punch landed, as if he had cracked the alien's skin. At the same time he felt a strong rush of pain travel up his arm. Ignoring it, he landed a blow on the back of the creature's neck. The creature fell forward. It looked as if it might fall, but it quickly regained his balance and, twirling gracefully on his left foot, he came back at Apollo with such force that he rammed the human against a control panel. Sparks flew all around the two battlers. Shocks from the broken panel seemed to burn through Apollo's entire body, and he felt his legs weaken. The creature took advantage of Apollo's momentary weakness, picked him up, held him over its head for a moment, then slammed him to the floor. As Apollo struggled to get up, the creature kicked him fiercely on his side. He fell back. Hearing Sheba begin to protest angrily to the creature, Apollo lost consciousness.

CHAPTER TEN

In his dream he saw the *Battlestar Galactica,* majestic against the dark backdrop of space, slowly pulling away from him. He tried to pursue it, his arms making swimming motions, but the ship quickly disappeared. He began to float in space. He began, he thought, to die. Then he was suddenly awake, and Croft was standing over him. Croft grinned crookedly, his usual look when he was cynically amused. Sheba stood nearby, gazing at Apollo with concern in her large eyes. Sitting up and looking around, he saw that they, along with the other conscripts, had been put in cramped quarters. Bunks were placed close together and people sat or lolled on some of them. Others paced a narrow aisle restlessly. Xiomara sat on a corner bunk, her face resolutely turned toward the wall. He looked back at Croft. There was a large welt, and some bruises, on Croft's face.

"I look as bad as you do, Croft?"

"No, it's like usual with you. You're the type tends to come through scrapes unscathed and unscarred."

Testing his body, Apollo remarked, "I sure don't feel that way. I hurt all over."

"Take it easy," Sheba said.

Apollo suddenly realized he felt none of the sense of motion that he associated with being inside an aircraft.

"We're not in their ship anymore," he said.

"Right," Sheba said. "We're in some kind of camp. Least-ways, that's what it looked like when we landed here."

Sheba held Apollo's hand and spoke slowly. After he had been knocked cold, she told him, all of the captives had been placed in an enormous dark chamber. Soon they could feel the ship descend. It landed heavily, knocking many of the prisoners against each other roughly. Soldiers came, and led them down a tunnel to an airlock, through which they were ushered, with many shoves from their guards, into the outside world.

Wherever they were, it was night there. That fact made it easier for them to make the transition from the total darkness inside the ship to the few flickering lights near the ship. Fire-light spread in a series of straight lines around and between hovel-like buildings. It had seemed to Sheba that, just outside the firelight, there was a lot of noisy and busy activity. How-ever, their captors hadn't give them much chance to look at anything. They pushed their prisoners roughly and quickly to one of the largest hovels.

"And they dumped us in here, and we haven't seen a one of them since. We haven't been here long."

A few bunks away there was a sudden outburst of angry voices followed by a small scuffle. Whatever the fight had been about, Beskaroon emerged the victor. As a sign of his prowess, he started pushing around someone else. Croft gestured in the direction of the altercation and remarked, "They've been like that since we got here. Can't sit still. Going to have to keep track of Besky and his buddies, especially in close quarters like this."

"Acknowledged," Apollo said. He glanced toward Xiomara and called her name. She remained looking at the wall as she responded.

"Yes?"

"Are you all right?"

"I'm fine. You're brave, all three of you."

"We're stupid, is what it is," Croft said.

"You are heroes."

"Heroes are just guys who don't know when they're losing."

"Oh, shut up, Croft," Sheba said. "This isn't the time for your jaded cynicism."

Croft's leathery skin seemed to redden slightly. He said nothing to Sheba, which intrigued Apollo. Croft was usually quick with a comeback when he was attacked. Yet at times like these, he could be distractingly human, even likable.

"Sorry, folks," Croft said, after a moment. "My brain's still a little loose from being knocked against the wall."

"Sorry I exploded, too," Sheba said.

Another minor miracle, Croft and Sheba apologizing to each other. They turned away from each other and sat down on their respective bunks. Apollo noticed a certain weariness in the way they settled onto the bunks. Their strength seemed to have been sapped. He didn't feel too strong himself. Had their battles on this strange planet taken that much out of them?

His thoughts were interrupted by the raucous ringing of a loud klaxon. The prisoners stared in puzzlement at one another. The klaxon rang again and a massive door at the end of the barracks was flung open. A long-necked creature strode in, followed by the lizardlike being from the ship.

"Off your butts, bozos," the long-necked one shouted. "You all look like swamp mud with fungus growing on it. A truly ugly sight. Stand up straight, scum. You're in the army now."

The long-necked creature's orders drew many moans and groans from the prisoners, many of whom were quite slow too stand up. The long-necked creature glanced shrewdly around. He selected Beskaroon as a prime troublemaker and glided toward him.

"Sarge," he said, addressing the lizardlike being, "I do believe we have a prime-grade specimen of vermin here."

Sarge growled something out of the side of his mouth. His nostrils vibrated fiercely.

"I can squash you, melonhead," Beskaroon growled. In exaggerated response, the long-necked creature put his hands on his melon-shaped head.

"Melonhead?" he said. "Oh, Sarge, we got a mean one here, for sure."

"Take care of him, Barra."

"Right."

"Right, melonhead, take care of me."

Barra's quick jabs and almost invisible kicks had Beskaroon

on the floor and in a daze in a moment. Croft took a couple of steps forward, leaned over Beskaroon, and said, "You squashed him good, Besky."

Beskaroon growled, then passed out. Barra turned his attention to Croft.

"And you, soldier. Would you like to try to squash me?"

Croft backed away, showing Barra the palms of his hands.

"Nope. I like the look of you, fella. Nice clean lines. And you're graceful. Very graceful."

Barra was not too strong on subtlety and could not figure out what Croft's mocking protest meant. Ignoring him, he began barking orders at his captives, telling them to form into two lines. The lines were shabby and Barra did his best to straighten them out, then he led them out of the barracks.

While the prisoners had been in their windowless hovel, day had come. It was a bright day, and rays of light glinted harshly off hundreds of metal surfaces. Nearby a platoon of mixed species was marching smartly, kicking out their legs with a sudden jerk, swinging their arms like stiff pendulums. In a field other soldiers trained with weapons. Apollo did not recognize some of the weapons.

As the double line of captives passed the marching platoon, many of its soldiers looked at them with scorn. Although it was difficult to discern words, several of the soldiers made sarcastic remarks, apparently criticizing the look and manner of the new recruits. Sheba, marching just behind Apollo, whispered to him, "What is this place?"

"Looks like a training camp to me."

"Training? What kind of training?"

"Basic training, from the look of it," Croft, who was marching in front of Apollo, said. "I think we're rookies again. Recruits. If you like, draftees."

"But that's insane," Apollo said. "They can't force us to—"

"We're here, aren't we? We've been recruited."

The prisoners were taken into a large building which turned out to be a single big room on the inside. They were led to a crude setup of chairs and ordered to sit. As Apollo settled onto his hard chair, he noticed a screen at the front of the room. On it now were flashing images which he soon recognized as war scenes. He'd never before seen so many different species at war with one another in mixed groups. It was even hard to tell which soldiers belonged to which side. Members of the same species were fighting each other. Instead of reptiles against amphibians, or humans against insectoids, each side appeared to be armies in which all the species were represented.

Sarge and Barra took up their positions on a podium in front of the screen, watching the rest of their captives file in.

"What do you make of those pictures?" Apollo whispered to Croft.

"Well, I don't think they're entertainment tapes, if that's what you mean. They need music for that."

When all the captives were seated, the pictures abruptly stopped and Sarge and Barra came forward to the edge of the podium.

"All right, scum," Barra shouted. "Button up."

It seemed strange to see such a comical-looking creature bark out orders. Perhaps that was why the noise level in the room did not decrease. Barra surveyed the chatting, whispering group for a moment, then he touched an area of his belt, which had on it more studs, buttons and other devices than the belts the prisoners wore. The talk in the large room abruptly ceased. Apollo realized that Barra had somehow made everyone stop talking. The controls in the belt could even do that. He tested it, tried to say something to Croft, and he found he could not utter a word.

"Okay, Sarge," Barra said, and the Sarge came forward. Barra shouted, "'Tenshun!"

As one, the captives stood and came to attention. Apollo could feel his body stiffening as the belt not only tugged at him but also tightened around his body. Barra surveyed the obedient group, and a grotesque line that resembled a smile crossed his face.

"At ease, scum!" he yelled.

Apollo felt the belt release his body and he abruptly relaxed. Standing at the edge of the stage, Sarge looked awesome. He had changed into a crisply tailored uniform on which was a colorful array of medals. On the screen behind him a set of circular and oblong symbols that Apollo thought might be a flag dominated the screen. When Sarge spoke, his nasal voice filled the room.

"I will be brief. You are all *volunteers* in the Army of the

Rightful Destiny. Our training period is brief. First you will be outfitted in proper uniform, be issued weapons, be given your training assignments and be initiated into basic training."

"Told you," Croft muttered out of the side of his mouth.

"Give up all your scumlike cowardly instincts. You are now warriors and will behave like warriors. Anything less will be considered treason. Some of you have obviously had experience in warfare. Your puny skills may do you some good in survival, but you must adopt our ways of combat. And you will."

Apollo thought he felt a slight tug on his belt, as if the article of clothing was deliberately agreeing with Sarge.

"You will remember that this is war! This is war! Every fiber of your being, every muscle in your body, every synapse in your brain will now be devoted to war! Don't expect a soft life and good food. I will work you so hard you'll want your eyes to fall out. I will demand so much of you, you will decide I am your new god. By the time I get through with you, you'll want to climb out of your skin and bury the rest of yourself. Those of you who have known suffering in your life, you don't even yet know what suffering is. I'll teach you suffering. You will hate me immediately, but it won't be hate yet. You will wish my death in thousands of repulsive ways, but you will not hate me enough. When I get through with you, then you will truly hate me, and then you will also be a soldier in the Army of the Rightful Destiny."

He stared balefully at his audience for a long while, a time during which the beginnings of the hatred he was demanding were surging within the new recruits. Then he turned his back on them, saying to his aide, "Barra?"

Barra snapped to attention himself while shouting, "'Tenshun!"

Apollo tried to resist the order but, as before, he felt his body stiffen. A few rows ahead one of Beskaroon's men managed to wrench his belt off his body. He climbed onto his seat, looking to left and right, trying to figure out what to do. Barra stepped forward, his stun-gun drawn. Coolly he took aim and shot the rebellious recruit. The man fell, knocking several chairs over. Soldiers rushed into the row, gathered the man up, and rushed him out of the room. Apollo noticed that the man was still alive. He glanced toward Croft, at least as much of a move as the belt seemed to allow. Croft looked worried, as worried as Apollo felt. Sheba, on the other hand, seemed quite relaxed. Xiomara seemed to stare at Apollo, but in that strange face of hers the meaning of the look could not be interpreted. Her face was twisted into an expression that could frighten children. Apollo wanted to reach out to touch her, but the belt prevented any kind of free gesture.

"Troops!" Barra called. "Left turn! March out by rows, back row first!"

The recruits were soon out of the building and on their way back to their barracks. Each was made to stand at the edge of a bunk. When the at-ease order was given by Barra, most of the recruits sank back wearily onto bunks. Croft came to Apollo, saying, "Well, Captain, what do we do now?"

"I wish I knew, Croft. I sure as hell wish I knew."

CHAPTER ELEVEN

Adama spent most of his time by the starfield, looking out. All of the search parties had returned now, all empty-handed. There hadn't even been a sign of Apollo's lost patrol, not even a pile of wreckage on some distant planet. Apollo was out there somewhere, with Croft and Sheba, and they would never be found. He had to accept that, he knew.

No one came near the commander. His subordinates who had had to approach him on routine matters had found him brusque and distracted. While they all knew why, and sympathized, it was easier to let him stand by the starfield while they took care of the *Galactica's* normal functioning.

Finally, the one man who always faced his commander fearlessly, Colonel Tigh, walked slowly to him and stood beside him quietly.

"What is it, Tigh?"

The commander's voice was toneless.

"Lieutenant Starbuck has requested permission to organize a new search party and go out again."

"Tell him no. We've done all we can do. We have to go on."

Tight wondered if he should advise Adama to let Starbuck have one more try. The brash young lieutenant sometimes had phenomenal luck. If he needed to, he could find a daggit hair in a pile of thread. At least, that's what they sometimes said about him. He also wondered if Adama was, as usual, putting too much store in regulations. Or was it the quest for Earth that was so preeminent in his mind? Must even the best men be sacrificed for it?

Adama seemed to read his aide's mind, for he said: "Our duty is to the fleet, Colonel. No single person, not even our quest, is more important than that. We must go to the planet Starbuck's squadron discovered and replenish both fuel and supplies. There's no other choice."

"We could still send out limited search parties, sir."

Adama's smile was bitter.

"To what purpose? To disappear themselves? We can't afford to be so frivolous with the lives of our pilots, Tigh. They're as valuable as the fuel, the —"

"But Lieutenant Starbuck—"

"Is needed for the mission just like any other skilled pilot. He's taken the same vows to serve the fleet as we have, Tigh."

"Yes, sir. But he does bend a rule once in a while."

"He's hot-headed, all right. Well, this time he's got to keep a cool head for a change."

"Aye, aye, sir. I'll tell him straightaway."

Tigh strode away in his usual crisp fashion. Glancing at his chronometer, Adama started his mental countdown of time elapsed before Starbuck confronted him. He decided it would be better for everyone if he met with the volatile lieutenant in his quarters.

Starbuck stormed into Adama's antechamber just as the commander settled into the chair behind his desk. Adama, noting the time on his chronometer, remarked, "You got here faster than I expected, Starbuck."

Ignoring Adama's pleasantry, Starbuck, in characteristic fashion, got right to the point.

"Colonel Tigh says I can't go out again."

"That is correct, lieutenant."

"But, Commander—"

"Believe me, Starbuck, I can figure this conversation out before you even try to speak your part. You demand to be allowed to continue the search for Apollo. There is still time.

There are still planets to be checked out again. You will go out alone, if that's necessary. You won't rest until you can find Apollo. You request permission to be detached to search-party duty. Does that about cover it?"

Starbuck looked away, some bitter tears in his eyes.

"Just about, sir."

"Good. Permission is not granted. Will there be anything else, lieutenant?"

Starbuck started to say something, then he stifled it.

"No, sir."

"You are excused then, Starbuck."

Starbuck strode angrily to the door, his back stiff, his body rigid. Adama called to him, "Lieutenant?"

Starbuck turned around, confronting his superior with angry eyes.

"Yes, sir."

"I am grateful for your devotion to Apollo. You have been a good friend to him."

The words did nothing to diminish Starbuck's anger. The two men merely stared at each other until Starbuck finally said, in a cold distant voice, "Will there be anything more, Commander?"

Adama wanted to say more but knew it would do no good. Not now, not while Starbuck was so bitterly angry.

"No, Starbuck. Dismissed."

Starbuck pivoted around in military fashion and left the commander's quarters. Adama sat back. He felt drained, and his sadness returned, as if flowing in to fill the empty emotional spaces. He wished he hadn't had to talk to Starbuck like that, like a commander to an ordinary subordinate. Starbuck was not ordinary. But it was necessary, in an emotionally charged situation like the disappearance of Apollo, to keep the volatile young lieutenant in check. Otherwise he would just find a way to go off on a personal search for Apollo. With Apollo gone, there was no better warrior on the *Galactica* than Starbuck. It would have been a shame to lose him, too, and especially on such a wild-goose chase. Responsibility had to win out. It superseded everything else, even personal quests and searches.

Starbuck had seemed to understand how necessary it was to attend to duty. But it was difficult to be certain about Starbuck. He would still bear close watching.

PART II

CHAPTER TWELVE

After the day's arduous training sessions with his platoons of raw recruits, Sarge found it necessary to relax. He relaxed as all members of his species did. He lay on his back, with only his well-articulated spine making contact with the floor. He had such a fine sense of balance that he could rest on his spine while rocking slowly from side to side. The rocking did much to induce the restfulness that he sought. While rocking, he spread his arms out in the air. They were not held there with tense muscles; instead, they were able to float in the air in much the same lazy way a swimmer allows his limbs to float on water.

The movements of his head also defied gravity. Using his neck as a pivot, he was able to move his head slowly in a circle without making any contact with the floor's surface. This movement was also easeful.

Sarge's species had practiced this type of physical relaxation for centuries. It allowed them to meditate on any subject. Sarge's meditation was so controlled that he could feel the air slowly rolling, it seemed, over his skin.

He knew he must review the training tapes for the day. But, since it had been an especially hard set of training sessions, in which he had pushed the troops energetically and relentlessly, he now had to work the tiredness out of his body before his review session.

To get his mind off his job, he concentrated on images of his family back on his home planet. In his mind he formed a wide group picture, with his many children and several wives arranged around him. Such a picture existed, on a mantel back home, but he had not brought a copy with him to war. His species did not believe in carrying the symbols of sentiment into duty areas.

He had not wanted to leave his family, but he had chosen the military as his career before his first marriage-triad and he had to go wherever his government sent him. His wives were wonderful ladies, cheerful and ebullient. He could not stand a female with moods, and there was some consolation for him to know that none of his wives were pining for him. They might think of him from time to time, and even send him a message through the proper channels of communication, but among the members of his species wives did not pine for soldier husbands. They had other husbands, after all, to occupy their social and reproductive times. Sarge had been told of cultures in which a single being was wed to another single being. It was a kind of marriage that he had much difficulty envisioning. Too many emotional ties could be attached to monogamous relationships. His species knew best. Every husband had several wives, every wife several husbands. It made the vagaries of life much easier to bear.

Sarge recalled each one of his children. He had fifty-three of the little demons now, and would have had more, if he had not been away at war for so many long periods of time. He had younger brothers, all of whom had chosen planetbound professions, who had more than double that number of offspring. When he was on leave, they sometimes made sly jokes about his small family. The jokes were meant affectionately, but sometimes he wished he had been able to stay home and form the kind of family that, in his culture, brought high status to its patriarch.

Sometimes he wished he could return home, collect his pension and live the sophisticated and uncomplicated life of a country patriarch. But his government was neither sophisticated nor uncomplicated. It pursued war rapaciously, wherever it could find it. Its leaders craved power. They loved the challenge of war and were willing to travel across half a galaxy to find it. Once there had been important goals, like the acquisition of territory and the bringing of primitive peoples into civilized society, but the goals were practically nonexistent now. The current war, at least, was like a game, the kind of game where unimportant pieces were pushed around a board in order for the important pieces to pursue certain strategies. The winning of a battle, a complete victory from a series of battles, these were now the important matters. The war now being fought on Yevra had started on another planet a few light-years away. That planet had been completely ravaged in much the same way Yevra would be by the time war left it. Sarge had been with this war since its inception, an inception that had probably taken place in a friendly back room agreement. He knew his side would pursue the other side to the end of the galaxy, destroying more planets along the way. Perhaps this time the war would reach the end of the universe. He had a recurring image of a battle at the end of the universe with its soldiers fighting their way into nothingness. Sarge no longer worried about the rightness or wrongness of the war. He could not even recall clearly the day when he had approached the subject of the war with any kind of intelligent thought. A large part of his life had been devoted to the war. He wished it could be over.

His thoughts shifted to the natives of Yevra. He had been attached to the early reconnaissance team which had scouted the planet during a truce period. The team's job had been to assess the possibilities of useful combat on Yevra. During the investigation, Sarge had had a chance to study the people of Yevra, their culture and their ways. He had discovered they were an innocent people who had rejected their own advanced technology for the joys of a simpler life. They had been untouched by any kind of war for at least half a millenium. While he could not have enjoyed living in the too primitive fashion of the Yevran natives, he had to admit that their contentment was admirable. They had adopted some odd superstitions, with which they controlled the potentially lawless in their society, but on the whole they were a people who did not deserve to have their planet destroyed by a war fought by invaders from elsewhere in the galaxy. If he had had the power of decision, he would not have involved the Yevrans in the war. However, the other side had fled to Yevra and were firmly entrenched. Sarge's side, the Army of the Rightful Destiny, had no choice but to engage the enemy in battle on Yevra. The Rightful Destiny armies had landed on Yevra and the war had been reinstated in earnest.

Sarge regretted that the rules of the war called for the recruitment of locals into the armies, whichever army got to the able-bodied types first. Both armies had been lucky that so many curious otherworlders had been lured to Yevra and abducted through the force fields that were always set up around the war. All of these draftees were necessary for the fighting of the war. It was so difficult to transport large armies across space that it had become essential to depend on recruits for hand-to-hand combat. The best warriors had to be saved for high-risk missions, the kind of missions that ultimately would turn the tide of the war to one side or the other. Still, Sarge thought, it was unfortunate that the recruits had to be conditioned to fight in a war for which they would have ordinarily felt no emotional involvement or commitment.

It was rare, he thought, for anyone to even care about the recruits. Perhaps he would not, except that he had to deal with them on a regular basis. He had to lead them to battle, watch them die. It was not a popular duty in his army, but he had shown himself to be suited to it long ago, and it seemed that now he would never be detached from it. They were all, recruits and noncoms, under the watchful eyes of the cold and distant officers who manipulated the war from impenetrable faraway bastions. The war had become little more than intellectual exercise for the officers. None of them had been in the field for ages, few of them even cared for the ordinary footsoldier. Mention the word infantry around them and they tittered while taking another sip of wine. Footsoldiers were merely pieces in the game. The war itself was all. The idea of acquiring territory was long gone. Who wanted the territory of the ruined planets they left behind? There was usually little left for the natives to rebuild. Sarge figured that the natives of the planets the war had already passed through were probably dying off, whole civilizations dying because of a war whose reasons were lost in obscurity.

When he started rehashing all the old stuff about the war, he knew it was time to end his relaxation period and get to the real work. He could never afford much time for relaxation, anyway. There was always too much duty. As always at the end of relaxation periods, it was time to review tapes.

He rocked himself like a cradle two or three times and then sprang to his feet. As soon as his feet touched the floor he began walking to his duty-cubicle.

In the cubicle, on a long table, were the several tapes representing the day's training. On each strip of tape was recorded the physical, emotional, and flashes of the mental activity of each trainee. These activities were transmitted to the tapes in Sarge's command headquarters from sensor-transmitters placed in series throughout the sweatband each of the trainees wore. The sweatband devices gained their power from the mechanisms of the belts. The belts controlled the trainees, told them their every movement, guided their skills, punished their resistance.

Sarge reviewed several tapes quickly, by donning a receiver-sweatband and pressing each tape against it. He did not enjoy this duty. In an instant he received not only the basic information he sought about the trainees' entire day, but he also got a sense of their pain and emotional turmoil. The negative qualities would decrease as the trainees became more conditioned. For the moment, they were the least enjoyable part of Sarge's job. At least he received the information from each tape so quickly that he did not have to dwell upon the pain and emotion.

He came to Xiomara's tape, put it on.

Xiomara's battle skills had sharpened at a rapid rate. She had become a most promising prospect in spite of the problems she created among her fellow soldiers because of her grotesque face.

Sarge did not understand why her face was considered so ugly. All their faces were ugly to him. *She had a special resentment for another recruit named Beskaroon. He not only hated her, he insulted her frequently and tried to interfere with her training.*

She hated this military life, but was compelled to continue to learn killing abilities. Her thoughts were frequently on a fellow Yevran named Trelon, an earlier recruit to the Army of the Rightful Destiny. Sarge remembered no Trelon. Apparently he was recruited into another outfit. Xiomara, he knew, believed Trelon to be dead. *She realized she was being conditioned and the unremovable belt had something to do with the control that was being placed over her, but she could not get it off no matter how hard she tried.* Sarge was impressed with how firmly she resisted the emotional conditioning of the belt, and yet how well she performed the physical tasks to which the belt guided her.

She had been assigned to the obstacle course today. Beskaroon, next in line for this training, managed to sneak into the course and hide behind a rock. Xiomara moved easily but cautiously through the first set of obstacles, then came to the area where Beskaroon crouched. As the hologram of an enemy appeared suddenly, jumping down from the large branch of a tree, Beskaroon flung a handful of dirt into her face. She nearly fell but, in the midst of her fall, quickly leveled her laser pistol and destroyed the hologram. After she hit the ground, she quickly rolled over past the rock where Beskaroon crouched and aimed her weapon at his face. Beskaroon stood stock-still, seeing his death about to emerge from the barrel of her lasergun. However, guided both by the belt and her own peaceful instincts, she twisted the gun just a bit to the right at the last moment and managed to fire a beam just past Beskaroon's left ear. He retreated rapidly. At the edge of the obstacle course, the observers laughed mockingly at him. It was clear from the expression on his face that he planned further revenge. Sarge was quite impressed by Xiomara's quick instinctive reactions. She was clearly ready for battle. Soon.

He removed the Xiomara tape from his sweatband and looked through a few other tapes. When he selected the Croft tape, he put it against his sweatband with some reluctance. He did not like being in Croft's mind, even for an instant. It was too foreign to him. He did not understand cynicism, especially human cynicism. He could be cynical himself, about the war at times, about his loneliness at other times, but his own cynicism seemed mild and insignificant when compared to Croft's.

Croft's adaptability to the training process and its conditioning was as good as Xiomara's, but it manifested itself in different ways. He had succumbed more to the controls in the belt and sweatband. He trained coldly and without much feeling for the others. Sarge did like Croft's coldness, although he hated to experience it. It was clear that Croft was the type who could be sent into the most dangerous combat situation with a good chance of surviving the experience. Croft, in a way, was the perfect trainee and would evolve into the perfect soldier.

Today Croft had been assigned to a combat simulation, one that required him to put the goals of the mission over the brutality of action. Sarge did not assign every trainee to this test. The experience of it, even when they failed, sometimes had too devastating an effect on the trainees' mental and emotional faculties. *Croft had been ordered into an encampment of nomads. The nomads were Yevran natives who had been hired to portray this tribe.*

Croft led a squad into the encampment. He had been told that the nomads were a tribe of noncombatants who had, however, conspired with the enemy to direct their fire toward the camps of the Army of the Rightful Destiny. He strode into the encampment with authority, giving orders out of the side of his mouth to his squad. Coolly, without much apparent thought, dutifully, he and his squad leveled their weapons at the peaceful-looking nomads and mowed them down with efficiency. As they fell to the ground, the faces of the nomads, who had not been instructed to expect this action, displayed fright and surprise. Sarge was impressed by Croft's emotionless attention to duty in this exercise. He had succeeded at the highest level of rating. In fact, Sarge knew, the exercise had been so successful that, afterward, when the nomads were revived, they all had long periods of disorientation, not believing that the weapons had been set at mild stun levels. They were all, in fact, convinced that they must be really dead. It would be impossible to use these natives for another exercise like this one. Sarge was quite satisfied with Croft's progress. Croft's partner, the one named Apollo, had already shown himself too compassionate to even be allowed to attempt this exercise. Apollo had significant abilities but strict obedience was not one of them. Yet.

Sarge considered reviewing Apollo's tape, but he was not ready yet to confront the strong personality of the determined and stubborn young man. He would have to check out the

Apollo tape eventually, but he needed some easier ones first.

He chose the Beskaroon tape next. Assuming the personality of Beskaroon, even for a moment, was a revolting experience, but the man's devious cruelty did make him good material for combat. He would be at least the kind of cannon fodder who would take a few of the enemy with him before dying himself. After the man's stupid trick on Xiomara, Beskaroon went through the obstacle course with efficiency. His skills were not as adept as Xiomara's, but he showed a brutal efficiency that Sarge admired. Still, he was relieved to remove the Beskaroon tape.

After a few routine tapes, he came to Sheba's. He was always a bit uncomfortable reviewing Sheba's tapes. Her emotionality made her a difficult trainee, although she had displayed sufficient battle skills. Sarge was not convinced she would make a good soldier. He put on her tape.

Sheba eased into her training exercise almost mindlessly. Sarge could detect very little emotion in her this time. She did not even seem to be thinking. He had noted that, in recent days, she had become more zombie-like. There was a strong feeling that she was just out to get the job done, to do what she had to before getting back to her bunk and sleep. *The drill took place at the firing range. She used a pistol developed by Sarge's species. The weapon was not well adapted for human fingers. One had to stretch one's hand to grip it. Nevertheless, Sheba handled the gun well.*

Her orders were to fire one of the explosive pellets with which the gun was loaded, then guide the pellet to its destination. The direction of the pellet could be changed by subtle movements of the soldier's fingers. Its course could be corrected to left or right, up or down. It could be made to glide, swoop, even make loops. The shooter could maneuver it to the exact spot on a target or the most vulnerable area of an enemy's body. The only way the enemy could dodge the pellet was to get out of its way with split-second timing. Even that did not save the target, since the enemy maneuver had to force the pellet to explode against some other surface. Otherwise, the shooter could make the pellet turn in a reverse loop and aim it at the enemy target again.

The pellet traveled at normal speed. However, the grip of the pistol contained an anti-chronometric device which, in effect, slowed down time for the shooter, who could then follow the pellet's path precisely.

The pellets Sheba was shooting in training did not contain a lethal explosive charge, so they only stunned their live targets. Most of these targets, Sarge realized, were soldiers from the front lines. Most of them were burned out and stricken with battle fatigue. Some of them would respond to rehabilitation procedures, but most would be sent back to the battle as cannon fodder. Even the rehabilitated soldiers usually did not last long when they were returned to the front lines. They never really regained their former abilities, but they were useful to the army because they kept newer troops from being killed prematurely. The whole war, Sarge thought, was run so pragmatically. Computer information rated who was expendable and who wasn't. The word went down, and the right soldiers were theoretically deployed into the right places. The expendable were put in vulnerable areas; the new trainees were put in relatively protected but good fighting positions; the best soldiers were assigned to roam the battle area, looking for the best shots and actions.

Sheba had a gun in each hand, and she used them with a deadly efficiency. She guided two pellets simultaneously and still managed to hit two targets at about the same time. She was a chilling trainee to observe, Sarge thought, so perhaps after all she would make a good soldier.

Putting the Sheba tape down, Sarge thought about the trio of human recruits who had come down to Yevra in their sleek airships. These three, and the woman Apollo had saved, would make an excellent team, a squad that might achieve wonders in combat. Sarge believed they all had abilities beyond what the average training leader usually saw, and he could make good use of them. After this training period, he was due to be reassigned to front-line duty. He wanted to take the four recruits with him. With him as their sergeant, they could make a crack fighting unit, an elite squad.

Like all careerists, Sarge wanted to move up the regular army promotional ladder. He had been in grade for too long, and it would be a waste if he didn't impress his superiors and move up in rank. Since his skill in the field would gain him the necessary combat-points to make him eligible for review by the promotion board, he believed that a unit that could function as a superteam would only enhance his possibilities. With these four, he could even, perhaps, get a commission as an officer.

He was not even sure he wanted to become an officer. Officers in his army had become world-weary intellectuals, governing the war behind their impenetrable walls, no longer seeing the war as a reality involving living beings. Still, he was getting tired of the dreary regimen of training troops and leading them in battle. Before his caution had always held him back from joining the officer ranks. Now he was ready to do something about it.

Nevertheless he must first attend to Apollo, the new recruit who showed so many leadership qualities that he threatened to take the shine of glory away from Sarge if he did qualify for Sarge's crack squad. Although it was rare for a humanoid to become an officer in the Army of the Rightful Destiny, Apollo could become one of the exceptions. Sarge wasn't so sure he wanted Apollo to become an officer, to outrank him. It might be better to allow Apollo to be killed during a military mission, get him out of the way at the right time. On the other hand, Apollo might be the key to the success of Sarge's special squad. In the training he pushed the others to performing well. It would probably be better to let Apollo survive, at least while he represented no danger to Sarge's ambitions.

Reluctantly Sarge picked up the Apollo training tape. He didn't want to review it, but his duty was to review the tapes of all the trainees.

Apollo had reached the most advanced stages of the training regimen. He generally passed each training test with the highest scores, even though he was continually trying to resist the demands put upon him by the mechanisms within his belt and sweatband. The noncoms in charge of each phase of training had had to increase the power of the mechanisms in order to force him to train properly. Sarge noted how delicate this aspect of training was. The trainee must be controlled through transmitted pain, but there could never be an excess of the pain. Too much pain could kill the trainee. But he had to order the highest safe levels of pain to be used on Apollo. The man was too skilled to be allowed to settle quietly into the general ranks.

*The noncoms had had to give Apollo heavy doses of pain
to make him perform skillfully today. The required exercise was
a survival drill involving the use of the laser-sling. Apollo was
taken to a nearby forest and forced to use the weapon on
animals. A large furry animal with long legs and a thin, twisted
horn had been placed by a stream where it was drinking peace-
fully. Apollo was ordered to kill it with the laser-sling. He
refused vocally, mentally and emotionally to disturb the life of
the peaceful animal. The noncoms, used to the man's resistance
to any logical order, increased the voltage of his belt and
sweatband. Slowly, fighting the moves every step of the way,
Apollo removed the laser-sling from its case. As the pain increased, so did Apollo's movements. He could not resist anymore. He twirled the sling a few times above his head, then
flung his "stone" at the animal. The stone, a compact force-
field generator, was guided to its destination by a laser setup
within the sling itself. When the stone detected the body warmth
of the animal, it immediately expanded and draped a narrow
force field around the creature. The animal, sensing attack,
bolted and butted its head against the wall of the force field.*
Sarge had helped develop the laser-sling. It was designed to
capture enemies and keep them within the force-field cage until
someone retrieved them. *The animal kept butting the wall for
a long while, until it had butted itself to death. It fell to the
ground.*

*Disgusted, Apollo clicked off the force field and went to
where the animal lay. To do so, he had to resist the strong pull
of his belt to remain where he was. He stood over the animal,
tears in his eyes. Gently, but with strong thrusts, he pushed
the animal into the stream. It floated for a moment, then sank.*

Sarge recalled Apollo's earlier puzzling actions with the
small animal which had been meant as sustenance for him. He
had disposed of that one, too. What was the compulsion of the
man to dispose of these animals ritualistically? How could one
species feel any emotion for another? It was a mystery which
Sarge could not fathom. It muddled his feelings toward Apollo
and strengthened his reluctance to have this superb soldier but
strange being in his outfit. He would never understand the man's
reasoning, he was sure.

*Apollo suddenly hurled the laser-sling into the stream. It
made some sputtering sounds, stirred up some water, then sank*

abruptly. The noncoms put pressure on Apollo through the belt to jump into the stream and retrieve the weapon. An unnecessary move, the Sarge thought. He could tell that the weapon had been ruined by the water. However, the noncoms had been taken unawares and their action had been impulsive.

Sarge flung the Apollo tape away with much the same gesture Apollo had used to get rid of the laser-sling. Turning away from the tapes, he started on the administrative work that was a necessary feature of the end of each training day. He began to record codes onto blank crystals designed to keep the statistics of training.

A low-pitched siren made Sarge turn away from his work. The code of the siren told him that Barra wanted to consult him. He released the locking mechanism of his door, and Barra swept in.

"Sarge," he said immediately, but with the proper deference, "could you spare some time to observe something with me? I don't know quite what to do about it."

Sarge was intrigued. Barra was rarely at a loss about anything.

"Of course, Corporal Barra."

As they left Sarge's quarters, Barra said, "I was just doing a routine survey and I saw Apollo with others around a fire and—well, you'll see."

"I look forward to it, Corporal."

CHAPTER THIRTEEN

Sleep. Just a few minutes of sleep. Then I'll be okay. Just climb into my bunk and—but no, got to keep going. If I fade out, all of them'll fade out. It's up to me to keep us from—from whatever is on the way to happen to us.

Apollo shook off the drowsiness and stared for a moment into the fire around which he had gathered everyone in the barracks. This campfire session, which he'd started only a few nights before, had become a part of the regular training for most of the trainees. After the first time, when he had had to roust them, they had become eager to take seats around the fire and listen to Apollo's soft and compelling voice.

Apollo saw weariness in every face. Everyone seemed to be weakening day by day, succumbing to the demands of the sweatband and belt. Apollo was quite aware of the control over them which those seemingly innocent items of clothing held. He had spent large portions of his break times trying to resist the gentle urgings of the belt and sweatband, but he had found that nothing seemed to budge them. He could not remove them, he could not counteract them, he could not even resist the majority of their commands. The clothing even seemed to control their dreams. At night the trainees had frenetic war dreams that were, in fact, clever distortions of the day's training as projected into them by the control belt. He had even noticed that the water in his nightly showers in no way affected either the belt or the band. Even while water was cleaning a warrior's body, it did not wet the controlling clothing.

Croft and Sheba's eyes seemed blank and listless tonight. If he lost them, how could he hope to save any of the others? How could he save himself? Croft, especially, seemed to have given up. The indomitable Croft, for whom nothing in the universe could be easily accepted, was becoming a mindless soldier. The transformation had no doubt been gradual, so that Apollo hadn't been able to see it until now. Perhaps, he thought, there was a similar listlessness in his own eyes. Maybe they were all becoming zombies. Zombies from whom intelligence and personality were being drained, like blood into a surgical bucket. It was possible that mindlessness was an objective of the training. What better kind of functioning soldier than one who had been turned into a zombie?

Much of his own military training had in its more civilized way been something like this zombie process, Apollo realized. Back at the academy, a certain kind of behavioral conditioning had been practiced. There were ways in which one was subliminally convinced to fight for the cause, ways by which glib slogans stirred vigorous emotional responses. But everyone in that training, everyone in service, understood how the conditioning worked. Soon most of them were engaged in passing it on, either by training new warriors or by going into combat. What happened in this strange training camp was worse. It insidiously laid the groundwork for total control of the individual. Once he'd realized the extent of the control, Apollo had vowed to resist it, and to help others resist it. It was their only chance for survival.

He glanced over at Xiomara. She stood on the other side of the firelight. The shifts in the flames did strange things to her already distorted face. There were shadows where there could not logically be shadows, bulges where he knew the contours of her face had been different. Her face did seem to alter from time to time, but this particular face, the one painted by the firelight, didn't seem quite real. He stared at it, hoping to see her real face underneath again, but it didn't appear.

Xiomara, while physically weakened, had been the most successful in resisting the control of the belt and sweatband. Her mind was clearer, her words more precisely spoken, her eyes (when Apollo could see them) more alert. He had started talking to her more and more, as the others became vaguer in their responses. Sometimes she talked of her life in the village, and he'd become fascinated with the ways of her culture.

Before everyone had arrived at the campfire, before the already seated could begin to doze off, Apollo began on a story. Since he'd initiated these sessions with strategy discussions which interested no one, he had quickly shifted to storytelling. He told the group tales of the war with the Cylons and the quest of the *Battlestar Galactica*. Tonight he had begun by telling them about Starbuck's adventure with the young warriors. His listeners were fascinated by the tale of a battle won with children as soldiers.

All during the tale, Beskaroon, who had become one of Apollo's most attentive listeners, edged closer to him until he sat at his feet. He looked up at him, his eyes wide and childlike, which was at least a change from their usual stupid slyness. When Apollo had finished the tale, Beskaroon said enthusiastically, "A good yarn, Apollo. Another. Please, another."

Apollo glanced around the group. Croft and Sheba's eyes were livelier now. These story sessions, invoking legends they knew well, evidently invigorated and comforted them. Even those who came from radically different cultures seemed caught by Apollo's tales of the *Battlestar Galactica*. The stories were definitely working, he thought, keeping personalities from disintegrating, keeping potential zombies aware. But could he keep it all up? Could he use the power of the word to save all of these trainees from disaster? Or would they just meet the death they were destined for?

The worst part was that he was weakening, too. The training and his struggle to keep everything together were taking a lot out of him. But he had to continue, so he began a new story.

"One time Lieutenant Starbuck of the—"

"Good, good," Beskaroon screamed and clapped his hands. "*Love* Starbuck stories. Go on, go on."

"Put a lid on it, Besky," Croft shouted.

Beskaroon stared angrily at Croft, who returned one of his

most obviously cynical smiles. The smile was, in fact, the most life Apollo had seen in Croft for some time. A bit of the old Croft that needed to be encouraged.

"You feel like another story, Croft?" Apollo asked.

"Suit yourself. I like to hear you talk about Starbuck, cap'n. You make him so vivid it's almost like the old bilge-rat is sitting here with us. I'm even beginning to miss him. And I didn't even like him."

"I thought it was me you didn't care much for."

"The both of you. Two sides of the same coin. Flip you, and it's hard to tell which one comes up."

"Croft," Sheba said, sighing, "you're full of soup."

"I wish I was. The swill they serve around here is corroding my stomach."

Sheba's eyes became wistful as she said, "I'd like one meal where I could separate its components into foods I recognize. Get our minds off this, Apollo. Go on with the story."

"Once Starbuck had his eye on this auburn-haired woman who was a shipping clerk in one of the supply ships."

"When didn't he have his eyes on some lady or other?" Sheba said. "Hell, you two aren't two sides of the same coin at all. Starbuck's eyes can't stop searching out women, and your eyes are blind to 'em."

At other times, Apollo might have been hurt by Sheba's remark. Still, she was not one to express her feelings and, in this camp, any life she showed was encouraging.

"The woman's name was Cyrra."

"Sounds like a disease to me," Croft muttered. Apollo ignored him.

"Cyrra was a young woman who'd lost her husband in a Cylon sneak attack on her city on the planet Virgon. She'd joined the fleet only after her family had also been killed in the final Cylon assault. A bitter woman, she was at first not interested in Starbuck's advances. There is nothing in the world that Starbuck hates more than being rejected by a pretty lady. While most men would quietly accept the rejection and bow out gracefully, Starbuck seems to thrive on accelerating his pursuit of romantic goals."

"Me, too," Beskaroon said. "Don't give up easy, I don't."

The others gave Beskaroon sidelong looks expressing their disbelief. It was hard to imagine Beskaroon in any kind of romantic state. His eyes were childlike in their rapt gaze.

"Well," Apollo continued, "it happened that Cyrra, in a routine tour of duty, was assigned to a mission on a planet which the *Galactica* and the fleet had stopped at in order to discover food and supplies. She was in charge of a fruit-picking detail on this apparently uninhabited planet. The orchard was situated at the foot of a mountain. I wasn't there, but I suspect that the orchard was colorful. I see it as even lines of trees, each with wide heavy branches. From each branch hung, in clusters, bunches of the luscious fruit we were seeking. I seem to recall that this particular fruit was red with purple streaks and, while its taste was evasive—a kind of sweetness that seemed to disappear immediately in your mouth—it was quite satisfying and full of nutrition.

"Cyrra, seeing that work was going well, went alone to a different part of the orchard to study the possibilities for harvest. Along the way she noticed that the trees on the mountainside of the orchard had less fruit on their branches. If she'd been more alert, she might have seen that the fruit on the upper branches had been nibbled on."

"Oh, oh," Beskaroon mumbled, "something bad's coming." Apollo grinned at his childlike reaction.

"Something bad indeed. It seemed there was a tribe of cave dwellers living in the various recesses of the mountain. And not just simple people. They were giants. They were twice as tall as our tallest men and women. How they ever squeezed themselves into normal caves is one of the most puzzling things about them. At any rate, two of these mountain people had come into the orchard, not knowing that some of our personnel were working there. They had stayed out of sight and watched the harvesting. Since they were primitives, all they saw was a group of intruders stealing their food. When Cyrra wandered off by herself, they saw their chance and grabbed her. They took her back to their cave home to show to the rest of their tribe."

Apollo's listeners were all wide-eyed now. His energy increased, knowing that he'd stalled the conditioning again, if only for a short time. His voice got more excited as he related how Starbuck, after other Galactican workers had been kidnapped by the mountain people, had gone off on his own to rescue Cyrra and the others. Following a pair of the mountain folk, he managed to sneak into their cave. Apollo's voice darkened as he strived to make the cave seem mysterious and mythic.

"Finally, Starbuck located where Cyrra and the others were being held captive. From a cliffside hideaway, he observed their ugly primitive cage. It was a large cave, with bars reaching almost to the ceiling of the massive cavern. The mountain people mocked them and tossed them food, then laughed when they scrambled desperately for it. Starbuck saw that Cyrra remained aloof, refusing to fight for food. She had become emaciated and her skin had the gray of death in it."

Improvising quickly, Apollo went on at length about Starbuck creeping toward the cage, then being ambushed by several mountain people. He made his audience moan as he told of Starbuck being hurled into the cage with the others.

"There was a moment when Starbuck, hungry now and just as desperate as the rest, was tempted to scramble for food along with them. But he realized that his captors were turning him into a primitive animal, a kind of being that they could understand."

Letting his voice become very dramatic, Apollo described Starbuck overpowering his larger jailers after feigning illness. Rounding up the other prisoners, Starbuck quickly led them out of the cage. However, they were seen before they could get to the cave's entrance and, running furiously, they had to retreat to the mysterious dark reaches beyond the area where the giants dwelled. They holed up in a sizable wall recess of the cave and quietly watched the clumsy giants' less-than-methodical search for them.

"After the giants had given up and gone back, Starbuck and the others realized they were in a desolate part of the cave without food, and only the water they could lick off the damp walls. The others, except for Cyrra, began to despair. They wanted to surrender to the mountain people, but Starbuck, of course, wouldn't allow *that*."

Beskaroon made a groan that nevertheless sounded like praise for Starbuck's action. Croft, in response, managed a sarcastic sigh. Apollo, amused and encouraged by the differing reactions, told his audience that Starbuck then worked out a plan, but refused the beggings of some of the audience to tell them what the plan was, saying that he would inform them of the plan at the right point in the story. *Whenever I think of it*, he thought.

His mind tiring, Apollo reached into deep recesses, which must have been like the cave he'd been describing, to finish the story. He also borrowed from a couple of mythological tales he dimly remembered from his father's telling of them when Apollo was a child. He told of how Starbuck and the other prisoners returned to the main living area while the mountain people were in the middle of a rest period. Few of the enemy were awake. They seemed wiped out by their heavy imbibings of mountain wine at the end of their search.

Starbuck, as Apollo told it, led his people right through the center of the cavern. On the way he liberated a pair of weapons from sleeping giants. The tiptoeing group wasn't even noticed until they got near the cave's mouth, where a pair of guards lazily stood. Using one of the stolen swords, he attacked the guards. Cyrra, with the other sword, was just behind him. Other giants were aroused by the fight. (By this time Apollo was emphasizing the word *giant* each time he used it.)

After he and Cyrra disposed of the guards, Starbuck waved the others on, pointing with his sword toward the opening and the open daylight air beyond it. The prisoners charged through the cave entrance. To give them time to escape, Starbuck battled with other mountain people who, now aroused, came hurtling toward him. Satisfied that all the prisoners were out of the cave, he dispatched several of the giants, then escaped out the cave opening himself.

Apollo was amazed at, and impressed by, the way his audience all listened eagerly now. He had brought them out of their doldrums, at least for a while.

He finished off his tale with a stirring account of how Starbuck came upon Cyrra halfway down the mountain. She had been grabbed by one of the giants and now struggled in his grasp. Screaming his famous battle yell, Starbuck jumped on the back of the giant and forced him to release Cyrra. He and the giant fought with swords and, after the giant had backed Starbuck against a big rock, Starbuck slammed his blade against the blade of his opponent and knocked it out of the man's grip. Frightened, the giant retreated back toward the cave. Cyrra hugged Starbuck out of gratitude.

"Back on the *Galactica*," Apollo finished, "Starbuck expected Cyrra to succumb to his charms. After all, he had saved her. When he next tried to romance her, Cyrra got this astonishing smile on her face as she rejected his advances. She explained that she still loved her husband and could not at this time belong to any other warrior. She spoke so warmly, so compassionately, that Starbuck, surprisingly, was pleased. He kissed Cyrra on the cheek and, with his famous wave, where his fingers seemed to ripple, he walked away."

Apollo stood up, his way of announcing the tale was finished. Many of the audience seemed sad. Apparently they wanted the storytelling to go on. Apollo wished he could continue, but he was too weary. He had barely gotten through the story's final sentences. Still, he felt satisfied, knowing that the session had delayed the army's systematic numbing of his comrade's brains.

Beskaroon patted Apollo on the shoulder and said, "That Starbuck's kinda dumb. Shoulda just took that gal for himself, he shoulda. Saved her life. Had the right to."

Xiomara muttered something under her breath. Beskaroon couldn't catch her words, but her scornful tone came through clearly.

"Keep it to yourself, mudface," he growled. He seemed about to insult her again, but Apollo's cautionary look made him back off. Croft laughed as he watched Beskaroon walk away from the fire.

"Never does get the point, that fella. Nice story, Captain. Kind of familiar, though. Reminds me of a couple of traditional Caprican legends."

"Well . . ."

"Yes, a lovely story," Sheba said. "Doesn't sound much like Starbuck, though, capitulating like that to the tender emotions of a woman."

"You do him an injustice, Sheba," Apollo said.

Sheba shrugged. When she spoke again, her voice seemed exhausted, her words disconnected.

"Maybe. I like the old bucko, don't get me wrong. I'm just glad he hasn't tried to add me to his string. I'm bushed. Thank you, Apollo."

Sheba joined the others who were now drifting away from the campfire. Soon only Apollo and Croft stood by the dying flames. Croft kicked at a smoldering piece of wood, knocked it back into the fire. There was an edge of bitterness in his voice when he finally spoke.

"You think you can get us through this, don't you? I can

see the old Adama-inspired dedication in your eyes. It shines through like the brass on a hero's medal."

Apollo stared at the place where the piece of firewood had fallen, watched it quickly turn to ash.

"What's your point, Croft?"

"My point, my *point* is that we've got about as much chance of getting out of this as a—as a—I can't even think of what. My mind is just barely functioning. I can feel my personality leaking out of me, like solium out of the fuel tubes of a decrepit freighter. What I mean, Apollo, is we got no chance. We got no hope. Remember when we climbed that mountain to get at that Cylon gun? Well, this is like that, only worse. We're trying to make our way to something we can't see, we're trapped here like we were in that blinding snow . . ."

For a moment Apollo couldn't speak. His thin long fingers rubbed his throat, as if trying to find the place where the words had lodged.

"But we got out of that trap," he finally said. "We got to the top."

"That's all that keeps me going. That we did it before. But that time at least we knew where we were, where we were going. We don't even know that now."

"Maybe. But remember the kind of warriors we are. We win over great odds."

Croft laughed. A good sign, Apollo thought.

"Odds? You're beginning to sound like Starbuck."

"Well, the old boy usually made sense."

"So what? You two can't blast us out of here the way you did it before. He ain't even here. I wish he was. I'd like to needle him, take a couple of shots at him. He's a great target. You, on the other hand—"

"Ease off, Croft. Don't let all this get you down. They want you to capitulate, that's what this is all about, that's—"

"Ah, can the pep talk, Captain. I'm gonna get some shuteye. Dream about facing a fire-breathing dragon without a weapon in my hand—at least in a dream like that I got a chance to find my way out. Not like here."

Croft muttered to himself as he meandered away from the fire. Apollo was tempted to call after him, to try to tell him that, as long as he gave his mind over to pessimism, their captors had him right where they wanted him. Croft would then be the perfect soldier, at least according to the way things were run in this training camp. But it would do no good to try to talk sense to Croft. He wasn't receiving sense these days.

Apollo stood by the fire for a long time before heading for the barracks. After he had left the fire, Sarge and Barra came out of their hiding place and watched him go.

"I see what you meant, Corporal Barra. This man, Apollo, is single-handedly keeping the others going with his tales of derring-do and romance."

"Yes, I thought it might be dangerous."

Sarge didn't speak for a moment. Instead, he found his own visions in the firelight.

"Dangerous?" he finally said. "Perhaps. It seems his idea is that imagination keeps the individualistic part of their consciousness alive."

"I think you are right, Sarge. I think he's doing just that. Shall I stop him? Order him to stop telling stories?"

"No. Keeping the troops from this might just stir them up, interfere with our duties even more. We can keep Apollo in line by having him devote a portion of his considerable energies to this . . . this storytelling. Storytelling never won or lost a war, Barra. We'll allow it to continue. Besides . . ."

"Besides what, Sarge?"

"Nothing, Corporal Barra, nothing. Return to your normal duties."

"Yes, sir."

After Barra had gone, Sarge continued to stare at the fire. It made shapes that he turned into the figures in the story Apollo had told. He wondered if he should have replied to Barra when he asked, "Besides what?" He would have said, "Besides, I like it."

CHAPTER FOURTEEN

Hera, who very much liked being taller than any man she was with, felt faintly uncomfortable at height differences between herself and other women. As she strolled now beside Cassiopeia, she was almost painfully aware of what a contrast they must make to the several men who walked by them and gave them a piercing but approving glance. While it was true that a more attractive pair of women could not usually be seen walking together in the corridors of the *Galactica*, they were an unmatched twosome. In addition to the height difference, they were unlike in the nature of their good looks, with Hera's features being strong and sharply etched, while Cassiopeia's good looks were softer. Hers was a more rounded face and her eyes hinted at subtleties that the eyes of the more direct and forceful Hera did not. Cassiopeia's light blonde hair contrasted sharply with Hera's lustrous black locks.

Hera preferred Cassiopeia's company more than that of any other Galactican woman, and they had hit it off well from their first encounter, an episode in which Hera had been deliberately browbeating Starbuck. Now Starbuck was a matter of concern to her for different reasons.

"So the old bozo's down in the dumps?" she asked Cassiopeia.

"Doctor Salik says it's a severe depression."

Salik had ordered Starbuck into Life Station, as was his right as the *Galactica*'s Chief Medical Officer, and given the young lieutenant a battery of physical and psychological tests. With pilots, he had explained to Cassiopeia, it was necessary to use the physical tests so the subject wouldn't balk at the psychological ones.

Hera sighed and shook her head.

"Hard to imagine Starbuck depressed. He's so . . . ebullient."

"Ebullient? Yes, I guess so. But that's only one of his moods. He can be pretty lowdown, too."

"Yeah, I heard."

For a moment Cassiopeia was taken aback at Hera's sarcasm, then she saw what the tall cadet had meant.

"Not *that* way! I mean, lowdown in his mood. Depressed, like the doctor says."

"Strange. It's about Apollo, isn't it?"

"What else? They were always close, the both of them."

"So are a lot of us. But we get over it."

Cassiopeia smiled. Whenever Hera saw that smile, she realized why the males of the *Galactica* were falling all over themselves to try to catch the pretty med-tech's attention.

"Well," Cassiopeia said, "you Vaileans do seem to have a healthy and positive outlook on life. But the rest of us, well, I don't know how to say it . . ."

"Life is hard?"

"Maybe. But for Starbuck it's not even that. He's got a great outlook on life ordinarily. At least, he's always been able to talk himself out of his emotional problems."

"The way he talks himself out of all kinds of trouble. Trouble like me."

"Uh-huh. But this thing with Apollo . . . they've been through so much together. They've saved each other's lives so often, it's like they're brothers, you know? They act like brothers and, well, Starbuck's got no family, except for Chameleon and who knows where Chameleon is now?"

Hera nodded. She had been there, at an airfield on a planet known as The Joyful Land, when a crafty alien named Crutch had abducted Starbuck's father, a wily con man named Chameleon. Starbuck had been through a heavy depression then, but he had worked himself out of it.

"And he has no other family," Cassiopeia continued. "After Apollo's kid brother Zac was killed in the Cylon ambush, Starbuck sort of replaced Zac as Apollo's brother. Then they became such great friends that, well . . . hey, is that Starbuck coming?"

"Yes. Better clam up."

Both women became so resolutely silent that they realized they must have looked odd to Starbuck. Hera tried to think of something chatty to say, but her mind was a blank. If Starbuck noticed their strained silence, he didn't show it. He was as glum as ever.

Starbuck was seeking a place to hide out, to keep away from all the people who were showing such annoying concern for him. He was also dead-tired from all the double duty he'd been pulling on the planet below. All parts of his body seemed to have already gone to bed and were merely waiting there for him to lie down and make it official.

When he saw Hera and Cassiopeia coming toward him, he had an impulse to turn and run away. His nod to them as he tried to pass by casually was blatant and perfunctory. Cassiopeia stopped him by placing a hand on his upper arm.

"Hello, Starbuck," she said amiably.

"Hi, pal," Hera said, grinning at him from over Cassiopeia's shoulders.

Starbuck didn't even reply. He just stood and stared at the two women. For a moment none of them could think of a thing to say. Finally Hera, setting her hands on her hips, spoke.

"I don't know about you folks, but I think the new Vipers lack the maneuverability and metallic tensile power of the old ones."

She stared at Starbuck, waiting for a response that did not come. She continued, "For all their improvements. Do you think our technology, based as it is on improvised methods, is on the decline, Starbuck?"

Starbuck merely shrugged.

"Or not?"

Another shrug.

"God, Starbuck, when did you die? I'm so sad I missed the funeral."

Starbuck's half smile was less than half like his former winning grin.

"Look, Hera," he said, "I'm not going to banter with you."

"No banter? My God, you *are* dead, bucko. A Starbuck without banter is like a Cylon without a red light."

The expression on Starbuck's face suggested to Hera that he didn't care what she thought. He started to walk on down the corridor. Cassiopeia called after him, "Anything we can do, Starbuck?"

"Nothing. Just leave me by myself."

Hera strode after him and spoke to the back of his head.

"That's exactly where you're wrong," she said. "Look, Starbuck, if you want to go off somewhere and cuddle or whatever hotshot pilots do with lovely young cadets like myself—well, pal, just want to let you know it's all okey-doke with me."

Both Starbuck and Cassiopeia were a bit put off by the eager young Vailean's forwardness, even though they'd experienced it often in the short time since she'd been aboard the *Galactica*. All Vaileans had a tendency to be open and forthright, and Hera had proven to be the most open and forthright of them all. When she had first arrived on board, she had pursued Starbuck vigorously. While he had been attracted to her, he had not liked her assertiveness. He had always preferred to be the one who made the romantic moves. He felt annoyed now that she had proferred the suggestion they cuddle up someplace. Hera seemed to like prodding him, confusing him.

Cassiopeia, who had come from a very ritualistic culture, found Hera's bluntness disturbing. Before she had found her niche on the *Galactica* as a medical technician assisting Doctor Salik, she had been a socialator on her home planet of Gemon. After the chaos following the Cylon attack on the twelve worlds, she had discovered that the citizens of other planets considered the profession of socialator as just one step above prostitution. They did not comprehend the intricate ceremonial distinctions, the strong moral rules that upheld the socialator tribe. As a result of her intensive training, she had come to believe that the kind of frankness that Hera exhibited publicly should only be found in private. Furthermore, she was more jealous of Hera than she cared to admit. Cassiopeia and Starbuck had once been an item. They had come close to actually going through the sealing ceremony that would have bound them to each other for life. However, Starbuck's recklessness and his wandering eye had eventually frustrated Cassiopeia and she had broken off their relationship. Lately, in his current pathetic and vulnerable state, she had begun warming up to him again. She wondered if she should let this aggressive Vailean take over action that should rightfully have been hers.

Starbuck kept his voice calm as he responded to Hera's proposition.

"Thanks, Hera. I'll consider that. Right now, though, I just want to stay alone."

Hera couldn't let Starbuck get away so easily.

"How about a drink in the Officer's Lounge?" she said. "I'm buying. We can drown away your sorrow together."

Starbuck's voice remained soft but became firmer. "No, but thanks, Hera. Drinks just make me sleepy. I'll—"

"Starbuck—"

Anger finally seeped into the tone of his voice: "Please, Hera, get off my back, damn it!"

He walked away. Hera made a couple of steps toward him, then thought better of this particular pursuit. She returned to where Cassiopeia stood, looking annoyed at everybody.

"Guess I overreached," Hera said.

"No," Cassiopeia said, "didn't matter what you said. He's carrying a load of grief on his back, and he can't find anywhere to put it down."

Hera smiled.

"Cass, dear, you need some practice in metaphor. On the other hand, I can't fault your accuracy."

There was a considerable emotional distance between Hera and Cassiopeia as they parted at the entrance to Life Station. In some way Hera couldn't define, Starbuck had gotten between them even in his absence.

When she realized she couldn't get Starbuck and his moods out of her mind, Hera searched the ship for him. By asking people she encountered if they'd seen him, she was able to track him down to the launch bay, staring at his Viper. The Viper shone oddly in the half-light of the cavernous chamber.

It seemed like an ornamental decoration.

Without speaking, she stood next to the gloomy pilot. She put her arm around him, squeezed his shoulders like an old friend. At first he shrunk from the hug, but she patted his upper arm and for a moment everything seemed all right. After a long while of sitting in silence, Starbuck said, "It relaxes me, hanging out here, listening to all the small sounds you can't hear anywhere else on the *Galactica*. The creaks and the metal groans. Listen."

Hera listened. In what had apparently been profound silence, she began to notice all the small noises of the ship. There were so many of them. They reminded her of a symphony played very softly.

"I see what you mean, pal."

Starbuck's head moved slightly, as if following the rhythm of the ship.

"You look exhausted," Hera said. "Why don't you sit down?"

"Here?"

"Right here."

His back slid down the wall until he was in a sitting position. Hera sat beside him. He rested his head on her shoulder. She couldn't think of anything to say to him, anything that would cheer him up. In a moment that didn't matter. Weary from his depression and hard work, Starbuck fell asleep. Soon Hera dozed off, too. When she awoke, feeling a lightness on her shoulder, she realized that Starbuck had gone. At first she thought he had abandoned her altogether, then she saw him at the controls of his Viper. She took a few cautious steps toward the spacecraft. He just sat there, looking ready to launch, his hand lightly on the joystick, his gaze on some far off, perhaps remembered, thing. She wondered if she should knock on the cockpit canopy, say something to him. No, she should not. She backed into the shadows and continued to watch him.

CHAPTER FIFTEEN

The war had not yet begun for Apollo. With his comrades, now fellow members of Sarge's Elite Squad, he crouched behind a thick bush and waited nervously for something to happen. Dampness from swampy ground seeped upward through his battle fatigues. His uniform was a dark green jumpsuit whose fastenings had been cleverly arranged to fit over and underneath the controlling belt which was never removed from a soldier. Apollo hadn't had his belt off since he had awakened on Yevra, even though he'd been through several changes of clothing.

Croft crouched next to Apollo. Xiomara was in back of him, right in front of Sarge, who was overseeing his elite squad with growing pride. By the end of training period, the efficiency and skills of this quartet had become so prodigious that he knew he'd not been mistaken in selecting them for his special squad.

Scattered in irregular formation all around the elite squad were other soldiers. While some trainees were apprehensively awaiting their first taste of battle, most of these soldiers were battle-hardened veterans. The veterans with exceptionally long service could easily be picked out of the group.

"For one thing," Croft commented, adding to a commentary he'd temporarily abandoned a few moments ago, "they never talk much. You don't talk much if you've been in combat long enough. And you notice their eyes? There's nobody living there, most of 'em. They're derelicts floating in eye-socket space. I tried to say something to a couple of 'em. They looked at me like nobody ever talked to 'em before. But that's not what scares me, Apollo."

"What scares you?"

"That these guys, they're *us* after a few days of fighting this damn war. This is ugly stuff, Captain. And it's our lives, from now on."

Croft's gloom had been increasing steadily. Apollo had nearly abandoned trying to cheer him up.

"Don't even think of it," he said now, laconically. "We're getting out."

Croft gave Apollo a sidelong glance that contained in it an abundance of his characteristic cynicism.

"Sure, Captain, sure. You're gonna be the hero of your own campfire tale and lead us out of here. You're just waiting for the best moment, then you guide us out of the cave. I know you heroes."

The sound that came from Apollo was somewhere between a sigh and a groan. The more he tried to help Croft, the more exasperating the man became.

"Croft, I don't know how we'll get out of this. And I have no big plans. But I know we'll make it."

"Sure, faith. Faith can burn fireproofing, that sorta thing."

"Never heard that one."

"You weren't born on Scorpia."

They stopped talking, each convinced there was no use trying to communicate with the other. Staring steadily ahead, they waited for the weird shapes in the mist to materialize into the enemy.

Sheba and Xiomara hadn't spoken since their arrival at this position. Each was poised, ready for combat. Xiomara wore a battle helmet low—purposely, so that it covered much of her face.

On Sarge's communicator, a small hexagonal metal device whose technology was mysterious to his squad, a signal sounded.

An odd scrawl went diagonally across a square screen at the center of the communicator. It seemed to mean something to Sarge, for his body immediately tensed. He crawled forward to Apollo.

"The front lines will form a series of wedges against the enemy," he said softly. "We're to slip through our own wedge and take out an artillery bastion that is supporting their left flank. It is tricky. The bastion contains amoebic diffusion-ray lasercannons set up in series. We're to go in low and kill all the operators of the artillery, then bring back a report on the weapon."

As Sarge spoke, Apollo's sweatband provided him the necessary information to comprehend Sarge's instructions. He recalled that an amoebic diffusion-ray lasercannon had beams that separated like the one-celled organism they were named for as they struck surfaces instead of passing through them. Each beam left the barrel of the cannon in a straight line; however, once it hit any hard surface it doubled, sending off rays in two directions. The lethal qualities of each ray were slightly diminished but still deadly after bouncing off the first surface. The newly formed beams would again divide as they hit other surfaces. Each time a beam was doubled, it lost some of its force, and frequently the beam which finally made contact with a living being was not deadly, but it was often disabling. Some rays which had been divided too frequently left little more than a brief numbness in their victims. At any rate, the hundreds of beams crisscrossing during a battle tended to stall forward movement.

"Squad, move out," Sarge ordered. Staying low, they moved toward the battle. At first they saw only soldiers moving cautiously. It was difficult to discern what was happening, but Apollo did see one soldier fall, apparently dead. The noise of battle increased as they proceeded further. Off to their left there was a fierce hand-to-hand battle going on. Just beyond that, a group of soldiers appeared to be pinned down by ordinary crossfire.

Suddenly an enemy soldier jumped down from above. He had been crouching in the dense branches of a massive tree. Both Apollo and Sarge whirled to confront the attacker, both firing simultaneously. The rest of the squad fired a split second later. The soldier, a thick-bodied creature with a birdlike face, fell dead. Sarge was proud of the quick reactions of his special squad. He had chosen its personnel well.

"Good shooting, Apollo," he said.

"Nothing to it. I didn't even think. It was automatic."

It occurred to Apollo that his choice of word was right. His reaction *had* been automatic, the response of a seasoned soldier to an ambush. He'd fired without a thought. The control exerted from the belt made his actions so much easier, a simple stimulus response. He could not have refrained from shooting even if some illogical prod of free will had cautioned him. The shooting had been necessary to protect the squad. However, the incident made Apollo uneasy.

The squad moved slowly forward through a foggy area. They heard troop movement on both sides of them but could see nothing. They could not even be certain whether the sounds came from their own soldiers.

They walked out of the fog so suddenly that they were taken by surprise. They had been prepared for the slow dissipation of the fog but not its abrupt end. It was hard for everyone to adjust to the new brightness, except for Sarge, whose vision could adjust instantly to any environmental change. After a moment, Apollo realized that the intense light wasn't daylight. It came from the maze of laser beams arcing and snaking across the battle, originating from the turrets of the slowly moving artillery bastion. Ahead of them soldiers attempted to close in on the bastion, but they dropped quickly, either killed or stunned by the intricate web of laserfire. The troops manning the bastion were able to pick their targets as the bastion edged slowly and relentlessly forward.

Sarge guided his squad around the right flank to an area untouched yet by the combat. From this new angle, Apollo saw the bastion better. It was mounted on several large wheels, whose rims bent easily as they went over rough terrain. The flexibility of the wheels kept the bastion upright. The barrels, which appeared when the pumping action of the guns projected them briefly forward through three narrow-slitted oblong holes at the front of the vehicle, were dark and shiny with no visible battle scars. The guns were fired in a steady rhythm, only one appearing out of each oblong window at a time. Croft crept forward to Sarge and Apollo and said incredulously, "We're gonna take *that?*"

"Yes," Sarge said. "Do you have doubts?"

"Doubts? Are you kidding? With you and Apollo leading the way, the rest of us can get our hammocks and swing and watch."

"I gather, from my study of your odd linguistic usages, that what you just said is sarcasm."

"Sarcasm? Me?"

"At any rate, I do not like it."

"I'm sorry. I was just named cynic of the month back at barracks, and I have to live up to the title."

Sarge eyed Croft suspiciously, wondering once again if the man, in spite of his considerable combat skills, belonged in the elite squad. It might be better merely to order him into the center of battle and let him absorb a full-impact beam. However, Sarge's training would not allow him to waste a soldier for such a skimpy reason. He had to use Croft until Croft was no longer usable. The way the man's personality was oozing out of him, that might be soon.

Sarge gestured his squad to crouch low, and then he led them around the bastion. The crouching kept them out of sight, and out of range of the laser beams, which could not hit low targets except on random deflections. It couldn't really zero in on any attacker who got close. Few ever got that close.

Sarge gestured to Xiomara, her signal to go forward. She hugged her demolition kit close to her chest. Since there was no entrance to the bastion, it had to be blown open. The gun operators, all of whom were the smallest soldiers among the enemy, squeezed in and out through the oblong gun windows. While the bastion was thickly constructed and could not be destroyed by explosives, Sarge had calculated that there was a good chance that a sufficient crack could be opened up in the bastion's side, at a point where the structure's two sections met in a seam.

Working swiftly, Xiomara planted the explosives and quickly retreated. When he was sure all members of the squad were ready, Sarge directed a thin blue ray at the line of explosives Xiomara had placed snugly along the seam. The bomb's action was slow and quiet. A slow-acting explosive was necessary for the materials with which the bastion was constructed. A fast one would have merely popped off, leaving only some black marks on the bastion surface. The slow action of this bomb, however, dissolved intervening material before opening a hole in the side of the bastion.

The bomb went off with a soft pop, and the squad watched as a narrow crack slowly crept up the side of the bastion. Apollo was surprised that the line was so straight and even. He had expected it to be jagged. The seam had parted enough for the members of the squad to squeeze through one at a time. Guided by Sarge's orders and the urgings of his control garments, Apollo ran to the bastion and, holding his body sideways, got through the opening. The room inside was eerie. Gun operators, who were just now becoming aware of Apollo's entrance, were extremely pale and emaciated figures. Their eyes were large and bulged out from their round bald heads. Their limbs were slim and delicate, looking like branches about to break. While they operated the guns with skill and strength, they looked like phantoms.

Apollo didn't have time to appreciate the scene's eerie aesthetics. The belt forced him to raise his gun immediately and start blasting away. He killed the entire battery of the middle lasercannon himself, while the rest of the squad, each coming through the hole shooting, took care of the rest. The driver of the vehicle, an especially emaciated fellow seated in the room's center, stood up, a weapon in his hand. Xiomara's shot tore open a large hole in his chest, and he fell over the octagonal wheel that steered the bastion.

Soon all the ghostly enemies were dead on the floor. Apollo, stunned, thought these so-called enemies seemed fragile, peaceful looking. He could hardly believe he'd killed beings so beautiful. Sarge clearly read the dismay on Apollo's face and recalled the man's compassion over dead animals. Would he always have this difficulty with downed enemies? If so, would he become as good a soldier as Sarge had expected? He crossed over to Apollo, stepping lightly over a pair of the bodies, and said to him, "They are Meyllians. Don't be fooled by their fragile appearance. They are a tough and hardy fighting breed and would have killed you in an instant, if you hadn't had the advantage of surprise."

Apollo looked up at Sarge, his eyes dazed.

"I understand, Sarge. It's just that—"

"Yes, I know. I had similar feelings once, before the war— well, before I saw what the war was all about."

"What *is* the war all about?"

"Winning. Let's get out of here before the soldiers outside recover and try to attack us in here."

"Too late for that," Croft yelled. He stood by one of the oblong windows and pointed out. Looking over his shoulder, Sarge saw enemy soldiers advancing toward the bastion.

"Is there any way we can get out of here?" Croft shouted.

"No," Sarge replied. "The way we came in is the only way out. It is the only way they can get at us, too."

"We can just pick 'em off then," Sheba muttered. Sarge was pleased by the fierce warlike enthusiasm in her voice.

"No," Apollo said. "We don't even have to do that. This is a simple vehicle. I can get us out of here."

Without asking permission from Sarge, he pushed aside the vehicle's dead driver and took up position in the driver's seat. Putting one hand on the steering wheel, he pushed forward a likely-looking lever on the vehicle's tiny dashboard. He guessed correctly. He could feel the vehicle lurch forward. Outside, the closest enemy soldiers quickly leaped out of the way.

"Look at 'em scatter!" Croft shouted.

Croft ran to one of the guns, studied it briefly until its principles were obvious to him. Sitting in the tiny gunner's seat, he began to operate the weapon. With one shot several enemy soldiers fell.

"Kobol bless me," Croft yelled. "I just knocked out seven with a single shot. This gun is astonishing!"

Apollo was disturbed by the fierceness of Croft's words. He was really caught up in this stupid war now. In one way or another, they all were. Croft's face looked insane, as he sat in the gunner's chair and squeezed off shots at the enemy. Xiomara, seeing the distress in Apollo's eyes, walked to him. The uneven and bumpy ride that Apollo was providing made her walk a bit wobbly.

"There's no way to stop him," she said. "He's not himself. He is controlled. We all are."

"I know," Apollo responded bitterly. "You think I enjoy zapping those guys?" He nodded toward the corpses on the floor. "Look, Xiomara, I've been in a lot of battles, but I always knew what I was fighting for, always understood the value of the war. But this war, it's—"

"Hush, don't excite yourself. We have no choices in what we do."

"There are always choices. We just have to find them."

"Then we'll do just that."

There was a hint of a smile on Xiomara's deformed face. He blinked and could almost see her real face. He wished they were alone together. He was drawn to her, in spite of the face her people had grafted onto her.

"Faster, Apollo," Sarge ordered. "There's smooth terrain ahead, and hundreds of the damned Pelters in between."

"Yes, Sarge."

Even as he responded to Sarge's order, he was disgusted with himself for his eager obedience to this bizarre reptilian leader. Nevertheless, as ordered, he pushed the vehicle to its limits and tried to ignore Croft's happy screams that followed each time he made a kill.

CHAPTER SIXTEEN

The battle was too large. It seemed to spread over too enormous a field. And Apollo stood right smack in the middle of it, gun in one hand, sword in the other, shooting in one direction, slicing in the other. Croft, Sheba and Xiomara all stood nearby, fighting their own battles. Their movements appeared to Apollo as slow, almost ritualistic. Sarge was at Apollo's side. Sometimes he picked up enemy soldiers by the throat and strangled them with one reptilian hand. They were a great team, Sarge and Apollo. If the enemy had any sense, none of them would come near the two superb warriors. Having Sarge next to him was like fighting side by side with Starbuck again.

Apollo shot down several enemy soldiers. They fell to the ground almost gracefully. Suddenly, as if emerging from the soil, an enormous creature materialized in front of Apollo. The creature was tall and wide, with a snout for a nose and reddish-brown fur all over its body. Its body was encased in a shiny armor and it wielded clubs in both its humanlike hands. It waved the clubs at Apollo, who felt a gale from the passing swipe. He tried to shoot it with the gun in his right hand, but the rays merely deflected off the creature's armor, so he started swinging at the attacker with his sword. The creature seemed to have no interest in the sword and didn't even react as Apollo ran the sword through the creature's leg. No blood or other interior substance appeared. The wound gaped open for a moment then seemed to reseal itself. Small bursts of steam squeezed out from the seam of the healed wound.

The monstrous creature now gaped at Apollo with hatred in its eyes. It reached for Apollo. Sarge tried to intervene but was quickly swiped aside by the creature, who grabbed both of Apollo's weapons right out of his hands and flung them away. Apollo, helpless, tried to retreat, but the creature picked him up and held him high above the ground. After letting some more hatred seep out of its eyes, it hurled Apollo up in the air. Apollo felt light as he reached the zenith of his arc, then fell into the creature's waiting hands. Again it tossed Apollo into the air and caught him. Apollo realized that the monster was merely toying with him. Then the creature threw Apollo as hard as it could and it was clear that he was going to let Apollo drop to his death. The ground rushed up at Apollo's face.

His scream as he awoke from the dream echoed back at him as he struggled to orient himself. He was sweating. For a moment he couldn't believe it had been a dream.

Xiomara sat on the edge of his bunk.

"Bad one, huh?" Xiomara asked.

"Afraid so."

"Anything I can do?"

"Get inside my head, fix the dream controls."

Her abrupt scornful laugh startled him.

"You don't want me inside your head," she said. "Enough monsters in there already."

"Don't say that. You shouldn't—"

She touched his forehead. Her fingertips were soft and warm.

"Shush. Don't trouble yourself trying to comfort me. Others've tried, nobody succeeded."

"Xiomara—"

"You say my name so beautifully. Nobody ever said it like that before. It has a sound, I don't know how to explain it . . ."

"Xiomara . . ."

"You don't have to keep demonstrating it. Go back to sleep. We'll all be getting up soon. Another day, another battle."

She stood and started to walk down the aisle between the double row of bunks. The sounds of everyone's sleep was a soft but irritating undertone of noise. Apollo sat up, swung himself off his bunk and ran down the aisle after her. When he caught up with her, he took her by her shoulders. He felt her tense up at his touch. He wondered if the flinch could be perceived in her face and what it looked like.

"I want to hold you close, Xiomara. I want to—"

"Let go of me."

She remained tense, her neck stiff, refusing to turn her face toward him.

"Xiomara . . ."

"That sound again. I could easily succumb to that, hero. Easily."

"Then—"

"Let me go."

The tone of her voice was so firm, so angry, that he released her at once. Slowly she turned around. Her body relaxed and she merely stared at him with no emotion in her face. He found he couldn't look at her. Even after all this time, the face was disturbing. He had not had a glimpse of the beautiful visage underneath for some time.

Xiomara spoke quietly, her voice a lovely counterpart to the unpleasant and unsettled noises of sleep all around them.

"Touch my face. Anywhere."

Apollo was startled by her words.

"What?" he said. "Why—"

"Just do it."

"I don't understand."

His arm raised, but too slowly and too weakly. She stared at his hands, which were now trembling. With a new strong effort he raised his hands toward her face, but she backed off abruptly.

"Don't bother," she said. "You hesitated. That was enough. I'd like to . . . to accommodate you, Apollo. But, funny thing, I don't like to be used. Really funny, huh? Sorry."

"Used? I didn't—"

"Maybe. Not in your mind. But, see, you didn't really want to touch me, not my face. You could touch the rest of me. I know I'm desirable that way. You could keep your eyes shut, see, you'd never know that—"

"Stop, Xiomara."

Apollo reached out, almost touched her. She saw his move and delicately stepped out of his reach.

"Say my name as beautifully as you can, it won't change anything. I won't be used, you have to know that. Don't worry, we're still friends, comrades in arms. I'd have liked to be . . . used by you, but I just can't. Get some sleep, hero. I'm going to."

As she started toward her bunk, the alarm klaxon blasted through the room. The discordant sound was a warning of impending battle.

"I guess I'm not going to," Xiomara said. "Inconvenient, this war."

At her bunk, she assembled her battle equipment rapidly. For a moment Apollo ignored the urgent threats of the klaxon and watched Xiomara, wondering to himself if what she had said about him was true. Why had he hesitated to touch her?

Although he tried to keep ignoring the klaxon, the belt wouldn't let him. He had to be ready for battle, too. He returned to his bunk and got his gear. All around him the other soldiers were throwing their equipment together, some of them looking as if they were responding while still fully asleep. Croft appeared to be especially groggy.

Outside the barracks there was an explosion. Nearly all the soldiers were knocked off stride, then there was a great rush for the entrance. Sarge and Corporal Barra squeezed by others in the doorway and began to roust the remaining soldiers. Barra hollered that the camp was being ambushed.

Apollo and Xiomara headed for the entrance simultaneously. Before going out, they looked at each other. Xiomara blew him a kiss. It was an odd gesture, carrying insult along with the affection. He saluted her, and she laughed.

They charged out of the barracks together. Right in front of them the battle was going on. Crouching slightly, they both shot at the same time. Two enemy soldiers fell and Apollo and Xiomara, responding according to their training as a precise fighting unit, plunged forward.

CHAPTER SEVENTEEN

Several battles later, Sarge's elite squad had become a slick
and sleek fighting unit, the best bunch of soldiers he had ever
collected together. Now, as he watched Croft efficiently lay
down a cover for the forward-rushing Apollo, he realized he
had never before seen a squad of warriors act so precisely
together. On a mission they performed in unison, knowing their
assignments and getting them done, protecting each other,
thwarting any counterattack.

If Sarge could have read Croft's mind, his confidence might
have been shaken. Even as he fired rapidly at anything that
threatened Apollo, he was only vaguely aware of what he was
doing. His mind was clouded, his memories of the past were
uncertain, his entire feeling of identity was shaken. The worst
part of his deterioration was that, in a small stubborn corner
of his mind, he was quite aware of it. And troubled by it. Once
in a while a clear view of his slavery would come through the
fog. Slavery? he thought. No, this is worse than slavery. Slaves
can escape, a prospect denied us.

The more time that passed, the less he even wanted to
escape. He was sure the others felt the same way. Each of them

was now inhabited by a strange kind of split personality. One
personality was the warrior—that part of them that was controlled by their belts and sweatbands. This side was a willing
servant of the state, even though they had no real knowledge
of what the state was all about. The only state they really knew
was the state of war.

The other side of their personality was that part of their
original identity that each retained. That was the part that was
quickly fading for him. Croft hated his own personal disinte-
gration. In the old days, the pre-Yevra days, he had been able
to see enemies as individuals. Now, accepting the dictates of
the controlling mechanisms, he saw this new set of adversaries
as inferior beings, as monstrous creatures that should be destroyed, as pieces of matter that shouldn't exist. In spite of his
famous role as cynic and pessimist, he couldn't stand feeling
all the hatred that had been implanted in him. He hated the
hatred more than anything else he had ever hated in his life.
Yet, though he strove to struggle against the hatred, he couldn't
fight it. He couldn't even speak to Apollo about it anymore.
Apollo, like the rest of them, seemed to care less and less with
each passing day, each passing battle. He was the strongest of
them all, yet he'd surely be destroyed eventually. They'd all
be shells soon enough.

"Look out, Croft!" Xiomara yelled.

Smoothly Croft whirled to see a human attacker bearing
down on him, a pair of laser pistols at each side, blasting away.
Croft ducked beneath the fire and, taking slow deadly aim, he
shot at the soldier. The shots opened a fiery hole in the enemy's
chest. As he died, his eyes had the same kind of zombie-like
look they all had. Croft hated that look.

"Why can't they even show some pain?" he muttered. He
rejoined the main battle. Near him Apollo was firing away
furiously, dropping enemy soldiers by the threes and fours.
Croft rushed to his side. As Apollo glanced confidently toward
him, Croft felt that surge of happiness that always came when
he and Apollo were functioning together smoothly.

Sarge watched Croft's quick moves with approval, and he
positively gloated over the skill of his squad. He hoped it would
never be broken up. Even as the thought occurred to him, he
wished he could take it back. Prideful thoughts often just pre-
ceded disaster.

Sarge didn't know how right he was.

• • •

Xiomara's back was against a boulder. Sheba, seeing her plight, united with her to repel a contingent of enemy warriors. Their concentration on the enemy was almost their downfall. A large, repellent, froglike creature in enemy uniform was slithering over the boulder. Reaching a long flipperlike tentacle down, it grabbed Xiomara's arm and pulled her upward. She slid up the rock, her legs kicking. Sheba screamed and took a shot at the ambusher. The beam just bounced off the armorlike coating of the creature's uniform. Apollo, alerted by Sheba's scream, ran toward the boulder. Seeing Xiomara in the creature's grasp, he took aim on its arm. It was a risky shot, but he hit exactly the target he'd aimed for. The creature yelled, a yell that was decibels louder than the din of battle, and dropped Xiomara. She slid down along the boulder.

As he hurried to Xiomara, Apollo did not see the trio of similar creatures emerging from behind the rock.

"Apollo!" Croft cried. "It's a trap!"

One of the froglike creatures, a tentacle waving in a large arc, threw a netting toward Apollo. The metallic thread of the netting gave off sparkling rays. It enveloped Apollo before he was aware of it and formed a kind of cage all around him. Croft remembered his instructions about this weapon. It was a capturing device. From a compartment at its top, a blue gas drifted out. Apollo's efforts to push the netting off him were in vain as he was made unconscious by the gas. His eyelids drooped as if he had just been reading for too long, and he was unconscious.

"No!" Croft screamed.

He knew what would happen. The creature, pulling the guidance rope of the netting, forcing it to enclose its victim entirely, jerked it toward him, and the cage containing Apollo began to sail into the air. The creature released the guidance rope as the cage picked up speed and flew upward. It disappeared so fast in the sky that Croft had not had time to think out what was happening. After it had gone, he knew the cage would ascend to great heights. In the rarified upper air, Apollo would try to breathe and the attempt would kill him. Then the cage would drop him to the ground with such force that his bones would be broken into tiny chips.

"It's—" Xiomara said. "He's—"

"He hasn't got a chance," Croft said. "Not a chance."

Xiomara was startled by the emotion in Croft's voice. He hadn't shown this much emotion at any time since she'd met him. Briefly, she put her arm around him but had to release him quickly to return to combat. Croft, with the aid of the belt, managed to come out of his doldrums and begin to shoot wildly at a new contingent of rapidly charging soldiers.

Sarge was astonished. One moment he had been mentally praising the skills of his elite squad in an inordinate fashion, and the next his best soldier was gone. While not an emotional individual, he did feel a strong sense of regret. He had liked Apollo, and such comradeship had been rare for him. He rarely liked the soldiers under his command, but there had been something in the human that elicited from Sarge a rare and grudging admiration. But it's war, isn't it? he thought. Everything in war is loss. Loss has to be accepted. He wondered why it was getting harder for him to accept such obvious things. Why did he look upward now and try to see the vanished Apollo? Why did he hope Apollo would fall out of the skies alive? He shook his head, uncomfortable with uncomfortable thoughts, and began barking orders at his now depleted elite squad.

CHAPTER EIGHTEEN

Among the crew of the *Battlestar Galactica*, it was said that
Commander Adama's voice could please a demon or agitate
an angel, and he didn't have to change an iota of pitch, tone
or emphasis to do either. Now, as he dictated his log in the
privacy of his cabin, the crewmembers might have been astonished at the new sounds of age and weariness that had come
into that famous voice. The loss of Apollo had hit him harder
than he wanted to admit to anybody.

He held the flat microphone in the palm of his hand and
spoke to it as if it were a miniature human being.

"This place—Starbuck's planet, as we've come to call it—
has proven quite rich in the materials we need. It is remarkable
that it seems to have no inhabitants. Doctor Wilker has spec-
ulated that the traces of poisonous elements in the air, enough
of them to force us to wear breathers at all times, are probably
too strong to sustain mammalian life at least. Nevertheless,
even with that information about the planet's unsuitability
broadcast widely throughout the fleet, the dissenters have come
to the fore with their usual monotonous demands to end this

long flight and settle on the—"

His dictation was interrupted by a soft knock on the door. He had heard that knock so often that he could always identify it as the polite rapping of Colonel Tigh. He hollered to Tigh to come in and the door eased open. Tigh entered, his arm lightly on Hera's elbow. She seemed to be trying to resist even this light pressure. A symbolic resistance, perhaps.

Hera towered over Tigh. Adama, standing up, realized that the young woman was two or three inches taller than he was.

"Cadet Hera, I presume," he said.

"Sir," Hera said, obviously trying to keep her irritation out of her voice, "with all respect, I demand to know why I've been brought here."

"I think you suspect. She was difficult then, Tigh?"

Tigh's smile was ironic.

"A bit. She spilled grog all over the uniforms of the arresting officers. It took three of them to subdue her."

Hera charged forward. Standing on the other side of the desk, she looked down into Adama's eyes. Her stare was unsettling, especially when coming down from that height.

"Am I arrested then?" Hera asked, unable to disguise the defiance in her voice. "Will you take me to the grid barge and lock me away?"

Adama smiled.

"Hardly," he said. "That can only come after a proper investigation and trial. And we're not about to take that route right now. No, I only had you seized because you have avoided all the routine summonses to report to me."

"Sir, with all respect, there are certain obligations that must be met ahead of *routine*."

The self-righteousness in her voice angered Adama and his next words were spoken harshly.

"Maybe on Vaile, but not on this ship!"

"Sir, with all respect—"

"Stow it, Cadet Hera! I'll excuse your insubordination on the grounds of your inexperience and because of the great help the people of Vaile have been to us. Sit down."

He felt more comfortable once they had sat. He liked being able to look directly at the young woman, across his desk, with all the command authority that the positioning implied, instead of looking up into her angry eyes. He nodded calmly at Tigh, a way of ordering him out of the room. Tigh exited saluting, and smiling. When the door had clicked shut, Adama spoke softly.

"Cadet Hera, the skills you've shown in your training have brought honor to all Vaileans. The—"

"Sir—"

"Please don't say 'with all respect' again."

"No, I wasn't intending that. I was going to be ruder than that."

"Oh? Then please, go ahead."

Hera was clearly the type who would cut her throat to prove the razor had a point.

"I just wanted to say that you don't have to soft-soap me. All that honor of the Vaileans felgercarb. You know?"

The comment, plus the childlike stubbornness in Hera's face, amused Adama, and he smiled warmly.

"I see you've picked up pilot slang along with your other achievements."

"I like it. It suits me. What is this all about, Commander?"

"About Starbuck. But you know that already, am I correct?"

"Correct, sir. And let me say, I don't spy on my comrades."

"I will not ask you to spy. Or inform in any way that's distasteful to you. I'm not a crusader, Cadet, just an experienced old officer who knows he's got a problem and isn't sure himself how to deal with it."

Hera was impressed by Adama's frankness. She relaxed for the first time since she'd been dragged into the Commander's quarters. He saw her newfound ease and his smile broadened. The smile was so disarming that she had to smile back. She had seen Adama often enough at a distance, but this was the first time she had spoken with him, and she was quite nervous. Most Vaileans had been taught to respect authority but also learned soon how to sneak around it as often as possible.

"Well," Hera said, casually pulling down the sleeves of her flight jacket, "I always liked a good sitdown chat. So shoot, Commander."

Adama leaned back in his chair. He liked this forthright young cadet and the tension of duty left his body.

"As I said, I wanted to talk with you about Starbuck. It has been reported to me that you are practically the only person he'll communicate with these days."

"He talks to me, yes. He's kinda surly about it, but he does chat me up a bit."

"What does he say?"

"I'm sorry, Commander, but—"

"Cadet, I know you think I'm leaning on you, but this is important. I don't know why I can see it, but I am sure that Starbuck's about to desert."

Hera was surprised at Adama's insight, a surprise that most people who served under the Commander experienced at one time or another when he showed his usual accurate perception of a situation.

"He's told you, hasn't he?" Adama said. "That he's going to take up a Viper and desert?"

"Sir, that would be—"

"Never mind, Cadet. The tone of your protest tells me it's the truth. Look, please believe me, I'm not trying to find evidence on which to build a case against Starbuck. I just want to stop him from making a mistake. I know he's grieving about Apollo and—"

"And you're not?" Her body pressed against the back of her chair as the Commander leaned forward. For the first time she was scared of him. "I mean, I thought Apollo was your son. You don't sound like a . . . a grieving father. I know Starbuck's grieving about Apollo and—"

She stopped speaking, to avoid betraying one of Starbuck's confidences. She didn't know what to say to the steely-eyed man behind the desk. She only wanted to get away. This dealing with command was certainly tough.

Adama spoke quietly. "I can figure out what Starbuck must've said. And it doesn't matter. How I grieve is my business. Is that right, Cadet?"

"Right, sir," Hera said, crestfallen.

Before he spoke again, Adama thought of all the sleepless rest periods he had endured since Apollo's disappearance, all of the private grief that had him staring at walls and seeing empty visions there. How could an outsider, like Hera, or even Starbuck, dare to judge his grief? Why did others think that their open grieving was somehow better than the internalized pain of loss? Starbuck was so wrapped up in himself that he couldn't see outside the borders of his own depression. Adama was not angry. Such blindness about grief was common, especially for the members of this fleet, all of whom had suffered similar losses. The pain everyone had already gone through had made it essential that the Commander not emphasize his own losses by displaying his grief.

"Hera, I have an order to give you." She flinched at the word *order*. "I see you are not keen on accepting an order just now."

"I'm afraid so, sir."

"Don't worry. I just want you to go on doing what you've been doing. Be Starbuck's friend. Perhaps your friendship will keep him from deserting."

Hera did not speak for a moment. When she did, it was in a calm and measured voice. "Sir, I'm not saying that you're right about Starbuck, but I must say this: Whatever is on his mind, I can't peach on him. We Vaileans are a loyal people, but we have certain codes of behavior when it comes to using official channels."

"All right, I won't interfere with that. I merely wanted to let you know that, if needed, I'm ready to help. However you deal with Starbuck or any other aspect of the situation, that is your choice, Cadet. I don't want you to, as you say, peach on Starbuck. But, if I can be useful, please call on me."

"I will, sir. If you can be useful."

Adama liked the forcefulness of Hera's replies.

"Exactly," he said, with similar force. "That will be all, Cadet."

"Yes, sir."

Hera stood up crisply and gave Adama a salute whose ram-rod neatness he had not seen from a pilot in ages. He could not help but return the salute just as smartly. Hera made a precise military turn and started for the door.

"Cadet Hera," Adama called after her.

She turned.

"Yes, sir?"

"I'm happy to have you aboard the *Galactica*."

She was clearly pleased, though she struggled not to show it.

"Thank you, sir. I'm happy to be here."

She left. Adama stared at the door, wondering if he had done the right thing with this forthright young cadet. Should he trust her? Was she too young to be allowed such trust? He wasn't sure, but his instinct, honed after years of commanding hordes of hot-blooded pilots, told him she'd be all right. Better than all right.

CHAPTER NINETEEN

Consciousness returned to Apollo in a rush, or perhaps it seemed that way because of the rushing air around his cage of netting. At first he was confused. This was so much like being abducted by the Sweeper recruiters that, when he looked up, he expected to see a recruiter, but there was no one bearing this load. He was merely going upward like a pellet shot out of an old-fashioned cannon. The speed of the netting capsule seemed to be increasing. There was no tactile sense of nearing a zenith.

The capsule had already ascended to such a great height that intense cold traveled his blood. He glanced downward. The battle was now far below him. He could not make out any of its detail. All he could see was a mess of movement and smoke and laser beams. It looked like a puzzle whose pieces had not yet been put together. For a moment he was fascinated by the view, then he realized, as the puzzle appeared to fall away from him, that he was ascending at a terrific speed. And accelerating.

In another rush, terror took him over. Not only was the air cold, it was getting thin. He could feel himself gasping for it and was not sure whether the gasps were caused by the atmosphere content or his own natural fear. If he kept going upward, he would be unable to breathe at all.

He pushed against the netted side of the capsule, to see if he could alter its course, force it to start its descent. At first he pushed lightly to make sure the wall was secure, then he tried to exert strength against it. He couldn't budge it.

His fingers were numbing with cold. At the same time another frigid patch crept up his legs. He reached back into his memory for the ice-planet training he'd once endured. He recalled an instructor telling a class about the importance of the shallow-breathing technique in rarified air. Shutting his eyes, feeling the floor of the capsule continue to push up against his feet, he tried to control his breathing. At first he couldn't get the hang of it, then he concentrated more fiercely, forced his body to relax and tried to ignore the growing cold, and soon he was shallow-breathing easily. He could still feel the sensation of rising and could tell that there was little air left, even for the restricted inhalation. The capsule was definitely slowing down now.

Then it seemed to come to an abrupt stop and to hang in the air for an excruciatingly long time before beginning to fall. Apollo continued the shallow-breathing technique as he felt the capsule pick up speed downward. When he could feel sufficient air permeating the netting of the capsule, he slowly returned his breathing to a normal rate. It was all right. There was plenty of air.

He looked down. The capsule seemed to be over a different part of the planet. There was no longer a battle below him. The terrain he did see was quite unfamiliar, dotted with a large number of lakes and abundant greenery.

The capsule was falling faster now.

"Great!" he muttered. "Now that I'm not suffocating, I can look forward to being smashed to pieces down there."

The capsule had reached such a height that he saw he had plenty of time to wait before his death. He looked for an escape. If he could cut his way through the netting, then perhaps he could jump free. But, no, that was ridiculous. Free of the capsule, he would fall at the same rate, be smashed to as many pieces.

Suddenly the capsule lurched slightly. At first he could not see what had happened. Then he saw a rip in the netting's fabric. Another lurch and another rip near the first one. The capsule pitched to one side, and Apollo fell backward against its wall. It pitched again, as if trying to dislodge him, and he was flung against the other wall, just next to the splitting fabric. The vent in the wall was larger now, he saw just before he was pitched the other way again. Before he could even attempt to regain his footing, the capsule tilted again and, his hands trying to grab at the rim of the netting, he plunged through the now enormous rip.

He began a long scream as he tumbled head over heels downward. He tried to straighten out his body to get a better view of the ground rushing up at him. Ending his scream, he knew there was nothing to do but make his peace with the gods and accept his death. He had never figured it would come this way, but then how could anyone plan the nature of his own violent death? He could not help but be frightened, but he realized that such a death was the normal fate of the warrior. He had seen many others die, had lost half his family to the war with the Cylons, so what else could he do? Still, he regretted meeting his demise in a brushfire war instead of the war for which he had been trained. He felt himself about to black out. If only he could black out before hitting the ground . . .

His eyes were on the verge of closing when he saw a new movement off to his right. There was something coming toward him. He couldn't make out its shape, but it was heading for him like a projectile. Perhaps it was a missile, about to blow him out of the skies. That might be a better fate than being killed by the fall.

As the shape neared, he saw it was not a missile. It was a living being. It seemed humanoid in shape.

For a moment the shape flew next to him, gently slowing Apollo's fall with his arms. When he had been safely decelerated, the figure took a tighter grip on Apollo's arms. Twisting his neck for a better view, Apollo saw, distorted, the figure of a blond-haired humanoid with pale shining skin and a sense of muscularity in his compact body.

The figure guided him toward a mountainside. They were flying slowly now. A section of the mountain opened up into a hole, or more likely a concealed cave. Apollo's rescuer slowed up their flight even more. The cave came up at them, and suddenly they were inside it, surrounded by darkness. Apollo recalled his entrance into the Sweepers' ship, which had also been a trip from brightness to darkness. This time the dark period was brief, and soon they were in a lighted cavern. Below them, other figures watched their approach. The blond figure gently settled the both of them onto the floor of the cavern. When his feet made contact, Apollo stumbled a bit, gained his footing, then turned to look into the eyes of his rescuer. His savior turned out to be a tall human who was already taking off the mechanical wings that had allowed him flight. His face would have been striking, except for the grim expression that seemed permanently etched there.

Ignoring the others, all of whom were watching Apollo intently, he approached his savior, hand out in greeting.

"Thank you, buddy. You saved my life."

The figure merely stared at the outstretched hand, his grim eyes seeming to disapprove of it. One of the people in the crowd stepped forward and said to Apollo, "He is mute."

Apollo turned toward the man. He was kindly looking, with deepset and intense eyes and a long, flowing dark beard with tiny streaks of gray in it. The robes he wore seemed to carry on the flowing lines of the beard. To Apollo, the man's most interesting physical feature was the way his skin appeared to be composed of patches of normal human skin that blended in graded shades to scaly areas that were as varicolored as mosaics. The mosaic patches might even have been aesthetically appealing except that their shapes were too odd and they were not placed artistically on the face. A mosaic area just under his jaw looked like the scar from a disease. It was certainly a strange face, compelling and repulsive at the same time.

"He can make sounds," the man explained, pointing to Apollo's savior, "but his people never developed a language and have shown no interest in learning speech. He is called Tren. Welcome to our settlement. My name is Razi Balzet."

Apollo stepped forward. Again he held out his hand and again it was ignored. Perhaps handshaking was not a custom with this group.

"Apollo. Captain Apollo."

"You do not wear the insignia of captain."

"I was not a captain in this particular army."

Razi Balzet watched Apollo drop his hand, then stared into his eyes. The look was complacent, as were the looks of others in the group, all of whom stared at Apollo laconically. Some of them wore outfits he recognized as enemy army uniforms. The sight of the clothing set off something in the belt, and he had an urge to attack that was difficult to control.

Razi Balzet apparently saw the tension in Apollo's body and realized where it came from. He turned and barked something in another language at a trio of the men in uniform. Immediately the soldiers began to move menacingly toward Apollo. He backed away, ready to deflect any attack.

"Don't be frightened," Razi Balzet said. "We want to remove your hostility toward us by removing the belt that controls you. Try to relax, make it easier for us."

"Stay away!" Apollo shouted.

The fierceness in his voice made the soldiers hesitate. Tren pushed past them. His face still grim, he walked to Apollo. Apollo was not sure what to do. He trusted Tren, yet the belt urged him toward his murder.

Tren lightly touched a point at the rear of the belt, a move that made it separate easily. Apollo remembered all the struggles he'd gone through trying to remove the belt and was amazed at the ease with which Tren had detached it. The mute man also, by reaching to a rear point, flicked the sweatband off Apollo's head. It drifted to his feet like a party ribbon.

With the two control garments gone from him, Apollo felt his body and mind relax. The weight of control seemed to leave him. He felt dizzy.

"The dizziness will stop soon," Razi Balzet said. "It has taken a great deal of power to control you. I judge you were not an easy subject. Most star travelers are not."

"Star traveler?" Apollo asked. His mind was slowly clearing.

"You came to Yevra from elsewhere. You and your . . . allies. In a very impressive trio of spacecrafts. We were just a fraction late in locating you. The other side claimed you first. The Sweepers, as they've come to be called. At any rate, they stole your vehicles as well as your souls. Too bad. If we could have studied your technology, it might give us an edge in this war. Well, no matter now. What can we do for you, Captain Apollo? Food? Rest? A woman of your species for your recreation?"

The dizziness made Apollo's speech a little fuzzy.

"I don't . . . don't understand why you saved me, why you would . . . would do anything for me. I come from the enemy."

"But you are not the enemy. An important distinction. You were recruited into their side, made to fight for them. Now you are on our side."

Apollo didn't like this last revelation and his anger was clear in his voice.

"What makes you think I'll fight for you?"

"We have our own . . . styles of persuasion, Captain. Not to worry. Accept the benefits we now offer."

Apollo surveyed the scene around him. He was surrounded. He remembered his own story of Starbuck's escape from the cave of giants. Could he find his own way out now? He had to. He had no desire to get embroiled in this stupid war again, not with either side. But he couldn't simply walk out of the cave, or even fight his way out. He couldn't do anything that foolish as long as there were larger concerns. Somehow he had to find an escape, go back, rescue Croft and the others, find their Vipers, and get off Yevra. The problem was complex. He had to wait for his opportunity to escape, and then seize it. In the meantime, he might as well cooperate with these people until he saw what they were up to.

"Well," he said amiably to Razi Balzet, "as soon as that belt came off, I started feeling this enormous hunger."

"And no wonder. The Sweepers feed you as inadequately as possible. Just enough to keep the fighting edge, not enough to keep you healthy. They don't give a hang about your health. All their soldiers eventually—when their fighting spirit is gone, and it *always* leaves them—become cannon fodder. Soon you also, Captain Apollo, when you had no more value to their war effort, would have been shoved to the front of the front lines as waste material to protect those warriors who still functioned efficiently. It is a blessing that we Pelters are not so cruel and dispassionate. We take care of our own."

Apollo knew that what Razi Balzet said about the Sweepers was true. Now that he was out of the belt, it was quite clear to him that, for the Sweepers, all war-weary soldiers were expendable. Each soldier was used by them till death. He would have died soon enough if he had not been captured. He would die as long as he was on either side of this vicious war.

It seemed to Apollo, who had lived all his life in times of

war, that wars never ended anyway.

Razi Balzet gestured elegantly, the movement of his arms sending ripples through his flowing gown. In answer to his gesture, servants came from the rear of the cavern, each of them bearing a tray of food. It was a feast. The food steamed, sending misty waves toward the ceiling of the cavern. It looked better than anything Apollo had seen in centons, or at least since his arrival on Yevra.

Razi Balzet clapped his hands three times.

"The feast will begin now. Come, Captian Apollo."

He led Apollo to a vast low table made of a dark-brown, smooth wood. Apollo was seated at the head, with Razi Balzet on one side of him, Tren on the other.

"Try some of this," Razi Balzet said, handing Apollo a plate of reddish-brown stew. "It is a Yevran specialty, a delicate blend of native fruit, vegetables and spices." Apollo took a taste. It was delicious. "And this to make it go down easily." It was a subtle wine. Apollo had never tasted anything like it. "We have more culinary wonders. Enjoy, Captain Apollo."

Apollo, not even conscious of the picture of voracity he was creating for the others, began to gorge himself on the wonderful Yevran food. Razi Balzet excused himself from the table and met with one of his aides.

"The food for the captain was prepared properly, I can see that."

"Indeed, sir."

"A couple of meals like this, with the conditioning drugs for his special ingredients, and we will be able to drug him properly, make him one of our own."

"Yes, sir."

"I think we can use this warrior to our advantage. Yes, very much to our advantage."

Razi Balzet recalled watching Apollo's arrival on Yevra, plus the several times he had observed the admirable warrior in the midst of battle. He had ordered Apollo's capture to use him for his own devices. The officers in the command bastion would be satisfied with his work, he knew. He was sure he would be promoted to a post in the bastion.

He strolled over to Apollo and bent down.

"Try some of the soup. It is superb, Captain Apollo."

He was overjoyed at the eager way the captain started spooning the soup into his mouth. Glancing over Apollo's head at Tren, he smiled with satisfaction. The ever-serious Tren showed no response to Razi Balzet's obvious happiness.

CHAPTER TWENTY

Each time Hera moved, she detected a new ache in her limbs. She'd been crouching so long, her arms pressed hard against her chest, that she didn't know whether she could straighten out at all. But she didn't want to shift her position too drastically and alert Starbuck.

Starbuck sat on the edge of his open cockpit, staring over his shoulder toward the launch tube. He was as sad as ever, as sad as he'd been since Hera had initially started observing him secretly, but in his face there was now a new determination. She was sure he was ready to make his move. At any moment, he might jump in that cockpit, rev up the Viper, and slide down the launch tube before anyone on the bridge could stop him. When he tried that, she would be faced with the hardest decision of her life. She was not sure where her strongest duty lay—to Starbuck as a pal or Commander Adama as her superior officer. Just thinking of having to decide frightened her. Ordinarily Vaileans believed that an individual should be given free rein—to follow a star, seek a goal, go for a victory—but this situation did not fit regular Vailean ideals. Starbuck's star was a futile one, the seeker was too valuable to the *Galactica* and the fleet, and there was no victory to go for.

Suddenly Starbuck shifted off the cockpit rim and jumped down to the launch-bay floor. He began to walk around his Viper. It was clear to Hera that he was inspecting it, perhaps for flight readiness. He stopped at the laser generator compartment, opened it, seemed to study the gauges inside. Shutting the compartment door with a satisfied look, he strolled to the other side of the vehicle. Hera couldn't see him anymore. She had to risk detection and move out of her hiding place. Edging cautiously along the wall, she tried to be as silent as possible.

She nearly jumped to the ceiling when, while passing a dark alcove, a hand reached out and grabbed her.

"Wha—?"

"Quiet!" a deep voice whispered. She turned and saw that her arm was being held by Lieutenant Boomer, Starbuck's wingmate and friend. Peering further into the alcove she saw that it was densely populated with *Galactica* flight personnel. Ensigns Greenbean and Giles, Lieutenant Jolly, Bojay, even Jenny, the ground crew CWO for Starbuck's squadron, all of them were hiding in the alcove.

"What the hell are you guys doing here?" Hera asked.

"Same as you," was Boomer's laconic reply.

"We're concerned about Starbuck, too," said Giles, who always spoke with youthful eagerness in his voice.

"We've been following him, too," said Jolly, his face for once not as cheerful as his name suggested.

"We seen you keeping track of him, too," Giles said.

"We've been watching you watch Starbuck, in a way," the petite but lithe Jenny said.

"The man is lucky to have such loyal friends," Hera commented.

"Yes," Jenny said, "but what good is it doing?"

"He's just been a-sulkin'," Greenbean said. The even-tempered ensign seemed unusually nervous.

"None o' us have been able to get a rise outta him," Giles said.

"He's in bad shape," said Jolly.

"You ask me," Boomer said bitterly, "he's about to fly."

"When?" Hera asked.

"Any time now. I've been his wingmate, know his moves. He's ready to disobey all orders, take off after Apollo. I can see it."

"Yeah," Hera agreed. "Me, too. I think he's ready. What should we do?"

"I say, go to the commander," Giles said, poking Boomer in the arm, "have Starbuck restrained."

"That wouldn't be—" Hera began, but Boomer read her thoughts and said, "I agree. We've got to stop him ourselves. We go through channels, he'll just go over the top, get mad and try again. Maybe we can talk sense into him."

"You ain't been able to do that up to now," Giles said. "How can you—"

"Can it, Giles," Jolly said angrily.

"Yeah, can it," said Greenbean.

"Ah," Giles scoffed, "you two guys always agree with each other."

"I'm with Lieutenant Boomer on this," Hera said. "Maybe, if he sees us, he'll at least think about what he's doin'. Honor of the corps and all that."

"Yeah," Jenny said enthusiastically.

"It's worth a try," Boomer said. He gave Hera an admiring look. "Now, do you think?" he asked her.

"Good a time as any."

The group slowly filed out of the alcove and, walking as quietly as they could, went around the Viper toward Starbuck. He didn't see them approach. He now seemed more determined than ever, ready to leap into the cockpit and take off.

"What's up, good buddy?" Boomer said softly.

Starbuck's first look was fierce and angry. He was ready to castigate Boomer. Then he saw the crowd of observers, and he became confused.

"Hi," he said, a little uneasy. "What're you guys up to?"

The glances that passed among the group might have suggested to him just what their mission was. Boomer stepped forward.

"Let's cut through the felgercarb, okay?" he said. "We've figured out what you're up to, bucko. We know you're figuring on deserting us . . ."

"Deserting *you?* I see, you're trying to personalize this. It's time to make old Starbuck feel guilty for leaving his comrades, hey? But you don't understand, Boomer, all of you. It's not deserting. I'm going after *Apollo*. I know he's all right. I know I can find him."

"Starbuck, stop fooling yourself," Boomer said. "Apollo's gone. We don't like that any more than you do, but—"

"How can you be so smug, so sure? All you guys."

"Starbuck," Giles said, "the Commander says—"

"I don't give a damn what the Commander says, or does, or if he raises his robe when he—"

"Don't go, Starbuck!" Jenny cried. Her voice had the sound of desperation in it.

"Oh?" Starbuck said, raising his eyebrows. "And why not, Jenny?"

Her voice became suddenly calm.

"Then I might have to work for one of these bozos. I don't cotton to that."

The remark at least drew a smile from Starbuck.

"Well, that's almost reason enough to stay. But I just can't."

"Boomer," Bojay said, striding forward from the rear of the group, "let's stop listening to him. Let's just shut him up and hold him down."

"Oh, Bojay," Starbuck said. "And how do you propose to do that?"

He had reached into the cockpit and come out with a pair of laser pistols, which he now aimed casually at the group.

"I know," he said. "You think I'd never use these on you. No, I wouldn't hurt any of you. But I don't mind giving each of you a good dose of stun. When you come to, I'll be history. So just let me go."

"Dry up, Starbuck," Bojay hollered. "You're not going to use those, not for any reas—"

Starbuck casually pulled the trigger of one gun and shot at Bojay. Bojay fell heavily to the launch-bay floor. Jenny immediately crouched by him.

"He's all right," she said. "Like Starbuck said, the gun's just set on stun."

"And the whole bunch of you can go to dreamland, all I care," Starbuck said, waving both pistols toward the group. "So just stay where you are, and I'll just take up my Viper for a little joyride. Good-bye, chums."

He started to step up to the cockpit. Hera, feeling her moment of choice plunging toward her, recalled her conversation with Adama. She didn't want to be a fink, but she did trust the Commander. She stepped forward.

"Wait, Starbuck!" she shouted.

"You're gonna make your play now, Cadet Hera?"

"In a manner of speaking. I want to go with you. I'll help you search for Apollo."

Her words startled Starbuck. He had not expected support from her.

"Why would you want to do that?"

"Selfish reasons. You know I got the hots for you, Starbuck."

"And you know why I haven't for you."

"Well, we can work it out. I won't make it difficult for you anymore. We'll do all things your way. I promise."

As she walked forward, her voice became deeper, sexier. It became the voice Starbuck had always wanted to hear. He had so many times been put off by her directness, by her making the proposition that, in his mind, were his privileges.

"Come on, Starbuck. We can let down the observation seat in your Viper. I can ride there right next to you. It'd be good to have two pairs of eyes to scan horizons, and I can fly when you rest—"

"Hera, I want to do this alone!"

"Stop encouraging him, Hera," Boomer called after her.

"Go suck a launch tube, Boomer. Starbuck, please let me come with you."

Starbuck hesitated. It *would* be useful to have help in the search for Apollo.

Hera now stood in front of him. Gently she pushed both his pistols aside and leaned closer to him. Her voice was equally gentle: "I'll really help, Starbuck. You won't regret it."

"Hera, I don't think—"

"I don't care what you think, pal."

Abruptly she jabbed her right fist upward, catching Starbuck on the point of his jaw. He fell back dazed. She grabbed both guns in a smooth maneuver and tossed them to Boomer and Giles, who caught them simultaneously. She smiled at the confused look on Starbuck's face.

"Sorry, pal. You missed this trip out."

As the other crewmembers rushed forward, Starbuck's eyes glazed over and he fell to the floor on his back.

"What do we do now?" Boomer asked.

"I think we need a strategy meeting," Hera replied.

CHAPTER TWENTY-ONE

Sarge did not ordinarily feel distress about anything, and so the feeling that had come over him since the loss of Apollo both disturbed and confused him. Suddenly the elite squad did not seem so elite anymore. It had, in fact, been falling apart. Sheba still responded to her conditioning but in an increasingly lackluster and mechanical fashion. Xiomara's stubborn ability to resist the belt's impulses had strengthened her. Unfortunately, her individualism made her less effective for the squad. And Croft was nearly a total wreck. Perhaps, Sarge thought, Apollo had held the squad together. It was not a pleasant thought for him. He should have been able to control the squad, with or without a single member. Perhaps he had lost his touch. Perhaps there had been too much duty in training camps, too many battles, too many losses. Perhaps he wasn't the top soldier he had once been.

Now the squad returned from a botched mission. They had run a sneak attack on an enemy encampment and been lucky to come away alive. The defenders had been ready. Sarge assessed the situation immediately and ordered a pullout. Even that had not been performed smoothly. Croft had not moved. Sarge had risked his own life to drag him out. When they were safe, Croft had not shown a single reaction to the escapade. Sarge got the impression that Croft stayed behind in order to get himself killed.

He considered dissolving the elite squad. Its members could be rested and retrained. If the new training did not take, they could be sent back to the front lines as cannon fodder. He always regretted making such decisions about fine soldiers, and he didn't understand why so many of them lost their motivation after several battles. Why did they become empty shells, prime targets for the enemy? It might have something to do with the conditioning. The conditioning might be too strong, too draining.

Still, these were only just questions in Sarge's mind. He did not truly understand the awesomeness of the conditioning. After all, nobody had ever needed to condition *him*. He was a natural soldier. Until lately, he had needed no convincing, no mechanical prods, to fight for his side. This group of humans had, however, shaken him up a bit. Some of their ideas, strange as they were, were appealing to him. He liked especially their bravery under stress and their apparent need to risk their own lives for each other. They were a puzzle, but an intriguing one, at least.

The squad marched far in back of him. He heard Xiomara attempting to talk to Sheba and wondered if they would have such a private talk if they knew his hearing was so keen, that he could hear every word. It had been an advantage to him to eavesdrop on them ever since the squad had been formed.

"Buck up, Sheba," Xiomara was now saying. "Things could be worse."

Sheba's reply was so laconic, it sounded phantasmal.

"Give an example."

"We could be dead."

"And you think that's worse?"

"Yes! I do! We've always got a chance."

"Tell that to Croft."

Xiomara glanced back at Croft, who was barely lifting his feet off the ground as he sludged along after them.

"Yes," Xiomara remarked, "he is kind of wiped, isn't he?"

"He's gone. There's nothing of him left."

"It's not that bad."

"Your opinion."

Xiomara stopped talking. What use was it anyway? Why did she even try to encourage Sheba and Croft? They were both unresponsive and pathetically sad.

She had, she realized, taken over Apollo's role in the squad, trying to keep it together and keep up its spirits. She wished she could tell tales of Starbuck around a campfire and give everyone hope, but they wouldn't accept either Starbuck or hope from her. An optimistic message, she knew, looked peculiar when emerging from her twisted face.

It would probably not be long before she succumbed to the despair that had captured Croft and Sheba. She couldn't figure out why she had resisted so long. The only reason she could think of was that she'd been through even worse before being abducted into this army. Her wretched experiences in the village and the horror of her reconstructed face still seemed more frightful to her than anything that happened in combat.

Perhaps she was losing ground. Whenever she tried to think of the old days, she could not remember what Trelon had looked like. She could only recall a few events of their life together. The rest was lost in a mental haze. It might not, after all, be too long before she went the way of Croft and Sheba.

Suddenly Sheba spoke. Xiomara was surprised to hear a rare note of emotion in Sheba's voice.

"What's the matter, Xiomara? You look so sad."

"It shows? I didn't think anything showed on this face."

"The face. What do you mean about the face?"

"Don't mock me."

"I wasn't mocking you, Xiomara. I haven't the foggiest notion what you're talking about."

Xiomara stared at Sheba and realized that what the woman was saying was quite true. Part of Sheba's personality breakdown evidently included an inability to see Xiomara's ugliness. Xiomara almost smiled, sensing the irony of this development. She could be a normal person among zombies. Wasn't that amazing?

"I'm sorry, Sheba. You *are* right. I was sad. I was thinking of my past. *Trying* to think about my past anyway. It wasn't coming through very clearly, I'm afraid."

"I know what you mean. I try to think of my father. He

was a great warrior. His name was Cain, Commander Cain. His exploits were famous. I can't remember any of them."

They walked a few steps further before Xiomara spoke again. "You miss Apollo, don't you?"

"Apollo? Who's he? He's gone. No point in thinking of him anymore. I don't miss him. I don't even remember who he was. He's just part of the body count now. Good riddance."

In spite of the trancelike tone that had returned to Sheba's voice, Xiomara noticed one thin line of tears coming out of the corner of her eye.

"He might not be dead. He might be alive somewhere."

"Yes. And daggits can fly."

"What's a daggit?"

Although Apollo was still alive, it would have been difficult for either Xiomara or Sheba to tell. The drugs that Razi Balzet and his crew had injected into him had turned him into one of the zombie soldiers that he had so often wondered about. When he was sufficiently under the power of the drugs, he had been given a quick session at the Pelters' underground basic training camp. It was quick because, as Razi Balzet had suspected. Apollo's skills were so honed he didn't even need the training. All he needed was the conditioning that would make him hate his former allies. He accepted the basic tenets of the Pelter Code excellently.

Now Razi Balzet and Tren watched Apollo chow down eagerly, his enthusiasm for Pelter food just as strong as when they had been giving him tasty stuff instead of the typical training swill.

"I like this one, Tren. Immensely. He can be a superior soldier, I can see that. What a fine animal! I will enjoy being his control."

Apollo was hardly aware of their concentration on him. He looked up once and caught Tren's eyes. Even though Tren maintained his grim look and Apollo his glazed one, there nevertheless seemed to be a momentary connection in the eye contact. It interested Razi Balzet.

"I think, Tren, you and this Apollo should be companions in combat. You'll make a good team, I suspect. Your assignment will be the usual this time. Enter the battle at any point that catches your interest. Guide Apollo. Protect him. But see to it that he cuts a wise swath through the enemy, one that our side can charge through. Is that clear?"

Tren nodded. When Apollo was finished with the meal, Tren guided him out of his chair. Tren was very good with Apollo, Razi Balzet noted. Apollo followed Tren's lead quite willingly. The two came to a stop in front of Razi Balzet.

"You're going to war now, Captain Apollo. Your mission is to break up enemy lines. And, by the by, to kill as many of the enemy as you can. With your considerable skills, you might be able to wipe out a whole battalion unassisted. From time to time during the battle, you will receive messages from me. They come through the receiver we have placed in your chest pack." The chest pack was also, Razi Balzet could have said, the device that would allow them to control Apollo from afar. "You will obey whatever I say. Is that correct?"

"I am your servant."

"Of course you are. That is all. Tren will lead you. Dismissed."

Tren and Apollo walked away, their gaits a little stiff, like proper automations. Razi Balzet was quite satisfied with himself.

Tren carried Apollo to battle in an odd air vehicle. It was flat with, it seemed, hardly enough dimension in its structure to contain any machinery. If Apollo had been himself, he might have wondered about how the vehicle operated. He and Tren sat inside a domed soft-walled canopy that rose tall above the vehicle. However the vehicle was operated, it flew along at great speed.

Silently Tren pointed. Ahead of them there was an enormous patch of smoke and fire. The battle. As they got closer, it was clear that the battle stretched across a great amount of terrain. While some of its activity could be seen from their high vantage point, it was difficult to pick out one side from the other.

Tren manipulated a soft bulb that evidently controlled the vehicle, for it began to descend slowly. At a lower height, Tren squeezed the bulb again and the flat vehicle began to cruise.

If Apollo had been able to see himself and understand anything about it, he would have been appalled. He looked exactly like the person he had dreaded becoming. His eyes were emotionless. They almost did not exist as a part of his face. His hair was disheveled and dirty. His mouth was slack and wet.

They could see individual fighting now. Apollo watched it lethargically. He remembered what combat had looked like and had no interest in it.

The ship, its landing guided by Tren's squeezings of the control bulb, landed on a clear patch of ground right in the middle of some furious fighting. Raising the bulb, Tren made the canopy fly off. He jabbed Apollo in the arm and pointed toward a section of combat. At first Apollo didn't seem to notice anything, then Tren pushed him forward, off the vehicle. Apollo stumbled before regaining his footing. Razi Balzet's voice came to him out of his chest power-pack, and suddenly Apollo enlivened. Anger came into his eyes, and his body tensed, ready for the fight. He drew his pistol and looked about for enemy, enemy to kill. He did not recognize that what he now regarded as enemy were once on his side. All of the soldiers, except for some differences in uniform and equipment, looked the same to him—in this battle or any other. He charged forward, already firing his pistol. Tren followed him, no approval for his combat eagerness on his grim face.

Razi Balzet and his aides watched the battle on a monitor. Their command position was some distance from the battle itself. They monitored Apollo's actions through the camera-transmitter attached to Tren's clothing. So long as Tren pointed himself toward Apollo, they could see him fight. And they were pleased with what they saw. Apollo was killing enemy soldiers left and right.

"There," Razi Balzet said excitedly. "Didn't I tell you this one would make a terrific fighter?"

"Correct," an aide said. "He certainly is a battler. A fine soldier."

"Perhaps we should get him out of the battle," another aide said. "Forget the test now. Protect him for a major mission."

"No," Razi Balzet said, his eyes fixed on the screen, where Apollo was dispatching still another Sweeper. "To be a full test, we must see him cut a wide path through enemy ranks. And there are tests I must try. Watch. Ooooh, look at that shot!" He leaned down toward a large bulb that functioned as a microphone. "Very good, Apollo. Now—look for the leaders. We must kill their noncoms."

• • •

Sarge had been ordered to proceed at once with his elite squad to a new area of combat. The order had come through his communicator from the damn officers who remained in their command bastion guiding troop movements and supervising the battle.

The squad moved quickly through their own ranks. Croft led the way. Sarge noted the unusual daring in Croft's movements. He was now convinced that Croft was trying to get himself killed. Well, he might as well. He had become useless as a part of this fighting unit. It would soon be time for Sarge to form a new elite squad from newer, more eager trainees.

They came to the area of battle where the fighting was fiercest. Sarge barked an order to Croft to approach by the left flank. Croft paid Sarge no regard and instead plunged forward, his sidearms blasting away. Ahead of him, enemy soldiers fell. Sarge tried to order him back, but Croft was not hearing, or not listening. Something had definitely gone wrong with Croft. It was possible his belt was malfunctioning or that he had just gone berserk and, by doing so, discovered the one way to counteract the belt's power. It was not unusual for an experienced soldier to go berserk in this army. Performing a reptilian equivalent of a shrug, Sarge ran after Croft.

Croft rushed into the battle, skillfully dropping enemy warriors all around him. Sarge had nearly caught up with him. A few of the enemy fell to Sarge's almost casual shots. Then he saw something that could startle even the usually unshockable Sarge. The warrior in the midst of the battle ahead was Apollo. Not Apollo as he had known him, but a nightmare version of him. His now evil face had been twisted into battle hatred. And he was killing what had been his own side in large numbers.

Croft yelled. It was clear to Sarge that Croft was heading right for Apollo. Sarge followed.

Razi Balzet's screen displayed a large portion of the battle. At the screen's center was the fiercely fighting Apollo. Razi Balzet was smugly satisfied at the success of his strategy. This human was indeed the kind of battler whose achievements would get Razi Balzet the promotion he so craved.

He almost yelped with delight when he saw Sarge rushing

toward Apollo. His fingers began to stroke two of the large mosaic-like patches on either side of his face, a gesture that came to him automatically when he was especially excited.

"Look there!" he cried. "I know that one. He has been a tremendous fighter, responsible for the deaths of many of our warriors. He's the one I want." He leaned down to the bulb mike. "Apollo, the reptile soldier slightly to your right. I want you to kill him."

Croft, running forward, shouted Apollo's name. Seeing Apollo had confused him, diverted him from his quest for suicide. Apollo was alive, but what was he doing here on the side of the enemy? He came to a stop not far from Apollo. Apollo ceased fire when he saw Croft.

"Apollo! What's wrong?"

In spite of his conditioning, Apollo recognized Croft. He also knew Croft was one of the enemy whom he must kill. To keep his arm from aiming the pistol at his former comrade, he dove behind the nearest rock and scrunched down. Tren, apparently remaining objective even about this extraordinary act, watched impassively, keeping his chest-camera firmly focused on Apollo. Apollo yelled without looking over the rim of the rock: "Get away, Croft. I don't want to hurt you. If they..."

"If they what?"

Croft had come closer to the rock. Apollo screamed and came scrambling over it. He had put his pistol back in its holster to protect Croft from him, but he could not help jumping at him, fighting him. To the onlookers it was a bizarre fight. Although both had fire in their eyes, each seemed to be pulling his blows, trying to keep from hurting the other. But, reluctantly, punches were landed, blood was drawn. Sarge came closer, looking for a way to break up the fight.

In the enemy's headquarters, Razi Balzet was screaming, "Leave that soldier alone, Apollo. The one I want you to kill is right next to you. See? Tren, help him!"

Razi Balzet watched Tren's hands trying to separate the combatants. He wasn't successful and, judging by the way the picture leaped toward the sky for a moment before again depicting Apollo and Croft, Tren had been pushed backward. Apollo was now looking beyond Croft, right at Sarge. Razi Balzet cried in encouragement, "Get him. Kill that stinking reptile!"

A strange sound came from Apollo's throat as he squirmed away from Croft. It was a dangerous sound, a sound filled with programmed hatred. His attention was no longer on Croft, who was again merely another insect among all the insect soldiers. He drew his pistol, aimed it toward Sarge, who was now aiming a pistol at him. Croft jumped at Apollo, screaming, "Apollo, no!"

Croft's quick move deflected Apollo's aim. The shot whizzed past Sarge's head. Croft looked back toward Sarge. It was clear that Sarge, cold-blooded soldier that he was, would now shoot and kill Apollo. Croft pushed Apollo out of the way. Sarge's shot whistled past both of them.

Croft was really confused now. The belt was sending him impulses of allegiance, while inside he recognized a higher allegiance to Apollo.

Xiomara and Sheba appeared a short distance to the rear of Sarge. Apollo, his composure regained, took aim again at Sarge. At enemy headquarters Razi Balzet was yelling at the top of his unpleasant voice, "Kill the reptile, Apollo! Kill him!"

Croft grabbed Apollo's arm, struggled with him. Sheba and Xiomara watched the struggle and could not figure out what was happening.

"That's Apollo!" Sheba shouted. "He's alive!"

Apollo grabbed Croft by the throat and took up a position behind him. He pointed his pistol toward Croft's temple.

"I'll kill him," Apollo threatened.

"That is immaterial to me," Sarge said coldly. He shot toward the two and hit Croft in the shoulder. Croft grimaced in pain.

"He's trying to kill the both of them," Xiomara said to Sheba. "He doesn't care."

"It's his duty," Sheba said calmly. "He must."

"Must?"

"And I must help."

"Sheba, that's just the belt talking, your conditioning, you can't—"

Coolly Sheba raised her weapon. Xiomara felt tugs from the belt urging her to dispose of Apollo, but she resisted them. She pushed Sheba sideways so that her shot was off the mark, then she jumped at Sheba and wrestled her to the ground. Apollo eased Croft downward, still using him for cover. At enemy headquarters, Razi Balzet was urging, "Forget that soldier, you idiot! Kill the other one!"

Apollo had to respond to Razi Balzet's urgings. He raised his pistol and shot at Sarge.

Sarge, hit in the side, fell to the ground and squirmed from the searing pain. His pistol was still in his hand and he aimed it toward Apollo. Tren, leaping forward, pushed Apollo out of the way of Sarge's shot. Croft, recognizing Tren as enemy, stuck out a foot and tripped him. He fell against Apollo just as Sarge shot again. The beam burned a line across Tren's back and he fell, face forward.

Razi Balzet, after staring at a picture where Apollo was at the center, watched the ground rush up at the camera, and then groaned as the screen became dark.

"What happened?" he yelled at the screen. "Tren, get yourself and Apollo out of there." The screen remained dark. "Tren!"

"I think he's been hit, sir," an aide said quietly.

"But what do we do now?" Razi Balzet said, his voice pathetic.

"We rely on you for such solutions, sir," his other aide said.

Razi Balzet felt defeated, but he kept speaking into the bulb mike, hoping to guide Apollo blindly.

"Apollo! Look around you. Find the reptile officer. Finish him off."

Apollo did hear Razi Balzet's command and he strode toward Sarge, pistol drawn, ready to finish him off.

Sheba pulled free from Xiomara and took aim at Apollo, muttering, "Must kill him, must."

Xiomara hit her in the back of the head with her pistol. Sheba passed out and fell.

Apollo now stood over Sarge, who was feebly trying to raise his pistol. Apollo kicked the weapon out of his hand. Sarge looked up at him and, when he spoke, it was in the same tone of voice with which he gave orders. "Kill me, Kill me now."

Now Apollo had two voices urging him to kill Sarge. He would obey. He would do it.

Croft, his wounded shoulder streaming with blood, came up behind Apollo. Apollo didn't see him. Croft knew he could not hope to overcome Apollo but, in the fight, had noticed the power-pack on Apollo's chest. Croft was good with devices, and he recognized the pack for what it was. With his last burst of strength, he surged ahead, his concentration on Apollo's power-pack. When he grabbed it, he pulled on it with all his might. As Croft wrenched it free, Apollo screamed in pain and suddenly knelt, clutching his chest. Some blood appeared between his fingers.

When the pain subsided, Apollo realized that his mind was clear. He remembered what the pack was and, instead of shooting at Sarge, he fired at the pack. Sparks flew from it and, with a sizzle, it stopped working.

Xiomara ran up to him.

"Apollo, are you all right?"

"Yes." His voice was weak. He tried to speak more forcefully. "Yes, I am. I'm free! I can feel it."

"I don't know what you mean."

Croft, breathing hard, holding on to his shoulder, said, "There's no . . . no belt . . . or anything else on him."

Xiomara felt impulses from her own belt. Resisting them, she said: "I'm supposed to arrest you, Apollo. Arrest you or kill you. I'm . . . trying . . . not to. Please go away."

"She's right," Croft said. "We're . . . still . . . still slaves. Nothing you . . . can do for us. Go. Get free. Off . . . this bloody . . . stupid planet. Go."

"I can't. Not without you. Let me try to help."

He pulled at Xiomara's belt, struggling to remove it from her body. An electric shock ran up his arm and he jumped away. Was there no way to remove the belt? He tried again and got an even stronger shock.

"Please, Apollo," Xiomara said. "I'm weakening. Can't resist. The power is too strong."

"Do what she says," Croft urged.

Sheba, conscious again, rushed forward. Her pistol was in her hand again. She stared at Apollo all the way.

"Traitor!" she screamed. "I'll kill you."

Her shot at Apollo just missed him, He looked at her, saw the murderous intent in her eyes. With a last despairing look at Xiomara and Croft, he ran off, reentered the battle, and disappeared. Sheba, her mind briefly clear, struggled to control herself so that she wouldn't chase after him.

"What did I do?" she said. "That was . . . was Apollo I shot at. I might have killed him."

"Well, you didn't, sweetheart," Croft said. "Let's go. We've all got work to do."

The sudden tone of command in Croft's voice startled both

women. He had been so despondent for so long that any energy from him was surprising.

"What about your shoulder?" Xiomara asked.

He glanced down at the wound, which still bled, and he said, "Forget it. It'll heal. Or I'll die. Doesn't matter."

They started to walk toward the point where the battle appeared to be the heaviest. Xiomara glanced down at the prone and unconscious Sarge.

"Sarge," she said. "What should we do about him?"

"He's dying," Croft said. "Fortunes of war. It'd be a waste of time to try to do anything for him. We have to fight now. Our orders. C'mon."

Reluctantly, Xiomara and Sheba followed Croft. In a moment, it seemed, they had returned to combat. Croft, strangely renewed, fought fiercely, as if he was imitating the Apollo he had just seen. Xiomara and Sheba, pistols drawn, joined him.

At enemy headquarters, Razi Balzet had left the control room. In an instant he had been demoted and booted out.

Sarge, slowly coming to, calmly listened to the fading sounds of battle. Testing his arm and leg muscles, he found he could move his limbs only a little. Even with this limited mobility, he made several attempts to get up. He could raise his head, but little else. Finally he gave up, deciding to die with the characteristic dignity of his species. Twisting his head he looked down at his wound. His blood had caked, and very little more was seeping through.

Waiting for death was boring. He tried to force it upon himself as if it were an entity that he could grab and use. He decided to just relax and try to empty his mind. Even trying not to think, he could not rid himself of the image of himself dying the proper soldier's death, slain on a battlefield. He had at least brought honor to his family. All of his children would have something important to remember about him.

At first he did not interpret the noises near him correctly. He thought it was an animal moving toward him, to examine him as possible food. Then he realized the noises were too steady. It had to be an enemy, looking to finish him off. The only way he could avoid such an ignominy was to feign death so convincingly the enemy would pass by him. He held his body still, which made him more conscious than ever of the dull pain in his side. He successfully restrained himself from grimacing and giving his pretense away. He felt the being's breath, hot on his ear. Then the being spoke, "You're faking it, I can tell."

"Apollo!"

"I've been watching you. Saw you move. Barely, but you moved."

"Why did you come back here? To watch me die? To finish me off, perhaps?"

"No. Thought I'd see if I could help."

"Help? Why would you help me?"

The gentle sound that came to Sarge's ear was recognizable as a human chuckle.

"My thoughts are free now. I kind of like you, fella. Anyway, I'm the one who shot you. I didn't want to, but I couldn't stop myself. You guys have got too many devices to control your warriors. I don't like that. Power-packs and belts, it's not fair."

"It is war."

"Sure, and felgercarb smells like flowers. I want to know about those devices, and where my Vipers are, and how to get off this damn planet, and I figure you for just the chap who can tell me."

"You think I'll tell you?"

"Well, I don't know that. But it's worth a try, Sarge."

"You want me to tell you now, as I die?"

"No, not yet. And I don't think you're gonna die. We'll find you some help. What works with guys like you?"

"If I could get to a river. There's a kind of herb . . ."

Apollo stood up, glanced around.

"Well, it's kind of a desert around here. Let's see what we can find."

Sarge tried to sit up, but this time was no more successful than he had been on his previous tries. Apollo, stepping into his line of vision, gestured him back.

"You can't walk. You'll start the bleeding again."

"And how do you propose I—"

"You just relax."

When he felt ready, Apollo leaned down and put his arms under Sarge's back. He was able to force the large unwieldy creature into a sitting position. With a few more adjustments, he abruptly hefted Sarge onto his shoulder. When Sarge's body was settled, Apollo asked, "You all right? The bleeding didn't start again?"

"I . . . I don't think so."

"Good, I'd hate to stain this marvelous new uniform your enemy gave me."

Taking a deep breath, trying to ignore the considerable weight of Sarge, Apollo started walking. After he had gone a few steps, he came to the still body of Tren. He kicked at it gently, hoping to bring the enemy soldier who had once saved him back to life. The body of Tren just shifted slightly at Apollo's kick. He was dead all right. Apollo regretted that. He would have liked to have known Tren better, but he didn't have time to mourn him. Making his hold on Sarge even tighter, he walked away from the debris of battle, hoping that a river would suddenly gush out of the ground.

CHAPTER TWENTY-TWO

Starbuck sat alone in the darkened Officer's Lounge. Moments ago, Tigh had come in and ordered everyone out of the room. The last one out had been Cadet Hera. She had blown him a kiss before departing. It was unusual, Starbuck thought, to be blown a kiss by a traitor. He rubbed his jaw where she had hit him. The woman surely did pack a wallop.

Perhaps he was being shortsighted in thinking of Hera and the others as traitors. They had, after all, gone to great lengths to do what they thought right. They really wanted him to stay on the *Galactica*. But he wasn't discouraged by their interference. He would go. They'd have to lock him up to keep him here. Even that wouldn't do. He'd find a way out of any cell, any confinement, any restriction. He had conned his way through life; his abilities wouldn't fail him now.

He would go.

"Before you go, I'd like to talk to you, Starbuck."

When he had gotten over his surprise at the way Commander Adama had sneaked up on him, Starbuck turned in his seat and said, "Ship legend's right."

Adama took a chair next to him.

"What particular ship legend is that?"

"One that says never to listen for the commander's approach. If he wants it that way, you never hear him even when you know he's coming."

Adama scratched his head, saying, "The crew does seem to like to impart supernatural powers to me."

"I think we believe you have them, sir." Starbuck stared amiably at Adama for a moment before saying, "And how did you know I was planning to go?"

"You left plenty of signs around."

"Probably did. Well, what are you going to do? Chain me to the *Galactica's* mast?"

"If I could, I would. But I know your determination, Starbuck. It's like a Viper without a pilot. Out of control, going straight, unturnable."

Starbuck lightly tapped the table.

"That's me, in a nutshell. Hot-headed Starbuck. Everybody's got the goods on old bucko. Transparent as a cockpit canopy." The muscles of his face seemed to tighten, and he said in a lower, grimmer voice, "I'm a lot more complicated than any of you think."

"I know that." Adama's voice was quiet and sure.

"Sir, please don't try to use psychology on me."

"It wasn't psychology. It was truth, or at least *my* truth. You seem to forget, I was a hotshot pilot once. I know the breed. Starbuck, I miss Apollo—so much I can't sleep nights, so much I'm not even running the ship well. Tigh's doing all the real work, while I gaze into the starfield. Been thinking a lot about the way I was. I used to take any risk, fly in when everyone else was flying by. I had to become less ... adventuresome when I assumed command positions, but I've never forgotten what the flying and risktaking felt like. I always knew I could die and somehow never cared. Now I have ... different feelings about death. Anyway, Starbuck, like all people on the verge of old age, I want something of my youth back. I want to know again, if only for once, what it feels like to be a, well, a hotshot pilot."

"I've seen your flying skill, sir. It's still considerable. Better than most of us."

"You mean I fly a shuttle with the best of them."

"Ah, you could probably outmaneuver me in a tight situation."

"Not quite. Nobody starbucks Starbuck, that's what they say."

"Except you, sir. Once in a while. Like when—"

"Starbuck, we're going out after Apollo."

It took a moment for Adama's words to sink in.

"We, sir?"

"The two of us. This is my bargain with you. We go out on standard mission regulations. I am in charge. When I say we return, then we return. I don't want any hotdogging flack from you, lieutenant. If we can't find Apollo, we both turn around and come back to the *Galactica.* Is that agreed?"

"I . . . I don't know, sir. That wasn't exactly my . . . plan."

"I realize that. But often we have to give up on a plan. This may be the time for you. Believe me, Starbuck, we will scour the sector. I won't give up easily."

"I believe you. I just don't know if I—"

"That's the deal, Starbuck."

Adama's voice was firm. Starbuck stared into his metallic blue eyes, knowing the commander always meant what he said. If Starbuck made the vow to follow orders on this one, he'd have to go through with it. He might be devious, he might be something of a con man, but his word was sacred. Finally, he nodded slowly.

"All right, Commander. Your way."

"Good, Starbuck, good."

Adama offered Starbuck the Kobollian handshake, a rare privilege. It was a fairly complicated ritual which began when the elder offered both his hands thumbs up and fingers spread. Starbuck accepted and finished the ritual with Adama.

"Initiate pre-launch procedures immediately," Adama ordered.

"Yes, sir!"

On the *Galactica* bridge, Tigh checked the monitors which displayed the scene in launch bay. Tigh was now in charge of the ship, command having been handed over to him by Adama only moments ago. Athena stood beside Tigh, who punched a button and, on central screen, enlarged a picture of Adama in the cockpit of a Viper. He was busily giving his launch CWO final instructions.

"He looks good," Athena commented. "Happy even."

There was a trace of anger in Tigh's reply: "Happy to be in harness again."

"You don't approve?"

"He's endangering his life. He hasn't flown a mission in—"

"I'm scared, too, Colonel. And I wish he wasn't doing something so foolhardy. But I'm proud of him, too."

Tigh smiled.

"Yes, I know what you mean. I think the whole ship has a feeling of pride about this.

In the launch bay the final preparations had been completed. Starbuck sat in the cockpit of his Viper, next to Adama's. Adama flipped on his interViper commline.

"Ready to launch, lieutenant?"

"Ready, sir!"

"Launch control. Open launch tubes."

"Launch tubes open."

Adama yelled the order to launch with the fervor of a young cadet. The pair of identical ships zoomed down their respective launch tubes and out into the darkness of space. While he noticed a few aches and pains that had never appeared before at initial thrust, Adama was overjoyed with the feeling of being in a Viper again.

For good luck, Adama and Starbuck flew their Vipers once around the *Battlestar Galactica* before heading off into the unknown.

CHAPTER TWENTY-THREE

The cool breeze and the freshness of the air made Apollo wonder if he had indeed so recently been a raving maniac about to kill his own comrades in a meaningless battle. Carrying the heavy load of Sarge across the battlefield, then through one ravaged field after another, before finally discovering unscarred ground and locating this river, had been laborious but had seemed to cleanse Apollo of all the evil warlike impulses that the belt on one side and the drugs on the other had instilled within him. The wind drying the droplets of water that had collected on his chest from his quick swim in the river seemed to cool his temper as well. Watching the quiet slow movements of some large antlered animals in a herd on the other side of the stream, he remembered how peaceful Yevra had seemed to him when he had first awakened in that meadow — so long ago now. He wondered how much time had passed since that day. Well, no use worrying about that now, he thought. Sitting on the bank of the river, he finished laundering his tunic in the cool clean water.

Near him Sarge slept. In repose, Apollo noticed, the reptilian creature looked different. The meanness in his face had vanished. In a way that humans could be said to look almost human, Sarge now looked almost reptilian. He made a soft humming sound, created by a slight vibration of his nostrils. Apollo wondered whether the sound was the reptilian version of snoring.

There were no new bloodstains on Sarge's bandages. Apollo had made the bandages out of the sleeves of Sarge's uniform. The quiet breathing sound and the absence of new blood were good signs that Sarge was on the mend.

Apollo finished his laundering and placed his tunic flat on a flat rock. Sitting back against another rock, he wondered how far the *Galactica* and the fleet had proceeded while he had been stuck on Yevra. It would be quite a challenge to try to find them again. Perhaps the Vipers, with their limitations, would not be able to locate the *Galactica*. Well, time enough to consider all that later. First he had to free Croft and Sheba, then find the Vipers. At least he was no longer under control, not by either army, so he was better off than he had been. There was some reason to hope, at least.

He glanced over at Sarge just as the reptilian creature's strangely sad and humanlike eyes opened. For a while Sarge merely gaped at Apollo. He was clearly disoriented.

"Feeling any better?" Apollo asked.

Sarge glanced at his wound and said, "Yes. There is little pain."

"Do you remember anything? How we got here?"

"No. You nearly killed me."

"Well, true. Sorry about that. I wasn't exactly myself. They have these drugs, see, they use for control and . . ."

"Yes, I know. The drugs were once outlawed. But you can't trust the Pelters. They are insidious. They will do anything to—"

"And won't your side do the same things?"

"No! We fight fair."

"You steal lives from people who have no concern with your war and you call that fair?"

Sarge grimaced from a sharp dose of pain that seemed at the center of his wound. He said: "We . . . need . . . soldiers. There are . . . never enough soldiers. We have to recruit them from . . . somewhere."

"So you just take over any planet you can use for the war and use its people, people who haven't even heard of war before."

"Don't be stupid. Everyone knows about war."

"Perhaps. But not everybody practices it as a way of life."

"Apollo—"

Apollo gestured, trying to wave away the argument.

"Forget it. My life has been devoted to war, too. Just like yours. I understand that part of it at least. What else do you remember?"

"I thought I had died. Then I looked up and, and you were there. You picked me up, didn't you?"

"Yes."

"And you *carried* me here?"

"You could lose a little weight, Sarge."

Sarge was genuinely amazed that Apollo would go to the trouble of lugging him away from the battlefield for the meaningless purpose of saving his life.

"How far did you carry me?"

Apollo shrugged. He reached down to touch his tunic, checking to see if the sun had dried it yet. It was still damp.

"I have a poor sense of distance," he said.

"But far. It must have been far. The war has not touched this place. You can tell. It reminds me of . . . of . . ."

Sarge was recalling his home, but he didn't want to admit that to this human.

"Of where, Sarge?"

"Someplace. I don't remember."

Suddenly he was asleep again.

"Oh, you remember," Apollo said softly. "I'm sure of that." He smiled.

The tunic now dry and feeling soft and fresh against his skin, Apollo lolled on the riverbank and tried to make plans. The ripples of the water seemed to emphasize the rippling aimless quality of his thoughts. He knew he wanted to rescue Croft and Sheba. He couldn't leave Yevra until they were free, too. And he wanted to save Xiomara, also. As he thought of her, an unsettling feeling came over him. He missed her, he realized that. He wasn't sure whether it was because he had come to depend on her so much, or whether he was falling for her. He imagined both her faces, the one he usually saw and the mysterious and beautiful other one that he glimpsed from time to time. He wanted to see her again very much.

Well, he'd have to get back to all of them. In doing so, he'd have to risk being captured again. If he couldn't find a way around the control their belts and sweatbands exerted, they might even be the ones to capture him. At any rate, their conditioning would make it difficult for them to act freely. It would be useful to discover how to remove the controlling devices. He remembered his abduction by the Pelters and how Tren had so easily flipped off his control garments. How had he done it? Couldn't ask him. He was just a part of the body count now. When he had been a soldier, Apollo had tried many times to remove the belt without success.

He looked over at Sarge, who had again come quietly awake. It was clear, however, the focus of his eyes was not on Apollo. He was thinking hard on something.

"A cubit for your thoughts," Apollo said.

"Cubit?"

"Money. We call certain of our coins cubits."

"And you pay for each other's thoughts?"

"No, that's just an expression. Sorry. Just asking you what you're thinking about."

"I won't give that out for free either. You *like* to know each other's thoughts?"

"Well, it isn't an overwhelming motive, but we do exchange our thoughts from time to time."

"That would be repulsive to me."

Apollo held up his hands, giving up.

"Whatever you say, Sarge. Let me check your wound."

He sat beside Sarge and reached for the bandage. In return Sarge swiped at his face. The blow caught Apollo on the side of his head, knocked him backwards, and momentarily dizzied him. Sarge sprang up and tried another punch. Apollo was ready for the attack this time and he dealt a rain of blows on the reptile's hard body. He could feel his knuckles being skinned with each contact. Sarge backed off, Apollo's blows and his own weakness forcing him to give in. He sat down again.

Apollo took Sarge's gun from behind the rock where he had hid it earlier. Gesturing with it, he said: "In case that isn't enough. I don't care to wind up trading blows with you, Sarge.

I can leave you here to die or we can cooperate. What do you say?"

"Cooperate."

Sarge's almost meek voice indicated his reluctance.

"Okay. I see I'm going to have to keep a good watch on you."

Sarge straightened his back. He was insulted.

"I said I would cooperate."

"Sorry. I know so little about you. Didn't realize your pride."

They didn't talk again for a long time. Sarge dozed off for brief periods. Once he awakened to find that Apollo had prepared a kind of vegetable stew out of edible material he'd located. He knew which plants were all right because a part of the training he'd received from Sarge had dealt with how to survive on native foodstuffs when detached from one's unit. After the stew, Sarge felt much better.

"Apollo," he asked, "why did you save me?"

"I was bored. It killed some time for me."

"Tell me the truth. You want me to cooperate with you, you must cooperate with me."

Apollo stared at the river a moment before speaking again. "All right. First and foremost, I couldn't stand by and watch you die. Especially since I'd shot you."

"Oh? You didn't want my death on your conscience?"

"Something like that. Oh, I can kill an enemy when the situation demands it, but I was out of my head, under their control. I saw you as an enemy, true, but only because my conditioning instructed me to see you that way. Just as the conditioning from your side makes your soldiers see their enemy as dreadful and evil beings."

"They *are* dreadful and evil beings."

"See, you're conditioned, too."

The spines along Sarge's arm seemed to change color, to a deep almost glowing green. Apollo sensed this was the look of anger for Sarge.

"I am not, as you say, conditioned," Sarge said.

"Really? Well, it wasn't forced on you as it was on us, perhaps. It just came naturally to you. At war long enough and it's easy to convince anyone that the other side is some scourge, some lower-than-low monster that must be annihilated. Our war is like that, too. Most of our people hate the Cylons.

Considering their viciousness, there may just be good reason for it, but sometimes I wonder what the beings in the metallic suits must be like. We rarely get to know any of them, you know."

Apollo relaxed and told Sarge about the war he'd grown up with. Much of his explanation of the war required him to talk about his father. He told about how the Cylons had ambushed a peace conference they had set up. He told how the Cylons had destroyed the twelve home worlds and forced the *Galactica* and its ragtag fleet on its long flight. He told of his father's quest for Earth.

"Sounds like a worthy goal, this Earth," the Sarge commented.

"Not everyone thinks so. We have a small war going on among our people, some on the side of seeking Earth, others who think we should pick any habitable planet and start our society there. My father keeps us going."

"He must be a great leader."

"He is. But even he has his doubts. I think he'd like to rest, give up the search. But something urges him on."

Sarge watched Apollo grow silent and waited a respectful time before speaking again. "I know that something. And I know the desire to throw it over and rest, also."

Apollo smiled.

"You have some doubts about this war?"

"Some? No, many. I had wanted to be an officer once. That ambition was revived when you and your companions became my squad. But I see now it was a futile dream. I am not officer material. I was always a footsoldier and will always—"

"You mention officers. I just realized, I never saw an officer in the field. Where are the officers?"

Sarge's sound was hardly recognizable as a scornful laugh. It was an eerie revolting noise. But Apollo had heard it before, in training, and he knew what it meant.

"The officers never come to the field of battle," Sarge said. "Perhaps that was why I wanted to be one, so I could get away from the war myself. The officers of both sides remain in their command bastions, guiding the events of the war with their devices, their machines. The only time you ever see an officer is when you are summoned to the bastion to be punished. And sometimes those who are punished never leave the bastion. I hate officers, Apollo. And, you guessed right, I hate this war. But I have always been brought up with the belief that I must do my duty. I always do my duty. Now you know about me. Are you satisfied?"

"It's not a matter of satisfaction. But I'm glad you told me about yourself. I gather that's a rare treat."

"Very rare. I never tell anyone about myself."

Apollo leaned toward Sarge. Sarge could sense the man's urgency.

"Will you help me, Sarge?"

"Help you? In what?"

"Well, initially, to free my friends. Croft and Sheba and . . . and Xiomara."

There was a different sound in the way he said Xiomara's name, Sarge observed.

"Xiomara. I was not aware she was one of your warriors."

"She isn't. But I've . . . that is . . ."

"You've grown fond of her?"

"Well, yes. You're surprised?"

"Surprised? Not at all. I am aware that some of your people regard Xiomara as having a disagreeable appearance. I know, for example, what the one named Beskaroon has done to taunt her. But I cannot see her that way, I see all of you the same. I cannot define differences. That should not surprise you. I know that you think of me and others of my species as ugly."

"Well, Sarge, I wouldn't say that."

"Would you say repulsive then? Repellent?"

"Closer."

"See?"

"No, I don't see. I was just joking. You are different to me."

"Well, others see me as ugly. I know that. Just as they see Xiomara in the same fashion. You are perhaps different, Apollo."

"No, not really. I see . . . ugliness. But it doesn't matter. It isn't important."

"You don't say that with certainty."

"I'm not certain."

Apollo became moodily silent. Sarge decided to change the subject.

"You were asking me to help you in freeing your friends."

"Yes."

"What do you need from me?"

"How to do it."

"Oh, an easy task then."

"You don't need to help me physically. I just need to know how to free them. How to get those damn belts off them. How to free their minds. The rest I can take care of."

"You are very confident."

"I'm, well, good at what I do."

"I can see that." Sarge felt the pain of his wound again and shifted to a more comfortable position. "All right, I'll help you. It is simple, anyway. There is a metal stud in the middle of a series of five metal studs at the rear of each belt."

"I've seen. I must have tried to work something with belt-studs many times when I was trying to get out of the belt.

"You cannot free yourself from your own belt. Another individual can, by twisting it one way, then the other, then the first way, and pushing. It's easy, really."

"And that's all."

"Well, you said you could do the rest."

Apollo grinned.

"Right."

"You know, I believe you can. And you know what else?"

"What?"

"I'm going to help you do it. I should be ready to travel by morning."

"Sarge, I don't know what to—"

"Please stop talking. I need to get back to sleep."

Sarge fell asleep instantly.

CHAPTER TWENTY-FOUR

Croft knew he had to die. This time out would be it, he was sure. He could hardly wait.

Xiomara watched him carefully. She would try to interfere, but he would outmaneuver her.

Funny how his will to die had made him stronger. Just knowing he would soon be out of this hellhole had invigorated him.

He glanced toward Sheba. He was sorry that, in his life, he'd never persuaded her to yield to his romantic proposals. What was really odd was that now he could have been successful with her. As she had declined in spirit, she had become quite malleable. Unfortunately, he no longer had the urge to pursue that particular quest. He wondered if he should make the attempt, just this once on the night before he would die, but he realized that even that small effort was impossible for him now.

Looking beyond Sheba, he noticed Beskaroon ogling her. Beskaroon had just been attached to the elite squad as a replacement for Apollo. Some replacement! The man would be an irritant to the squad if they could work up the energy to be irritated. They were all too listless to pay much attention to the loutish Beskaroon. Even Xiomara ignored the several insults Beskaroon had made about her face. Instead of deteriorating under control, Besky actually had become stronger. He thrived on it. He loved the shooting and killing that the controlling garments forced him to do. It was hardly force with him. Perhaps he was merely a survivor. A total rat, but a survivor.

Croft hoped that, after his own death, Beskaroon would not be successful with Sheba. Ah, it didn't matter. After he was dead, what would he care about what Sheba did? Looking at how the life had gone out of her formerly bright eyes, he decided that she probably wouldn't last much longer in this army anyway. And what if she and Beskaroon got together? What a cosmic joke that would be, after all, the kind of joke that justified Croft's cynicism.

Barra, who had been promoted to sergeant in place of Sarge, strode into the room. He didn't like what he was about to do. Orders had come to him that the elite squad would be sent out on one more mission. Barra had been told to make sure that the old members of the squad did not return from the mission. Obviously, the command staff had given up on the elite squad and now wanted to use it for enemy target practice in one of their complicated battle plans. Well, Barra thought, there was no need to question command decisions. He only had to carry them out. The new member of the squad, Beskaroon, would be allowed to live and then transferred elsewhere. Easy to understand that, Barra thought. That kind of soldier could be placed anywhere and still maintain the same kind of stolid utility.

Barra walked along the line of bunks, using a club to hit the footstand of each one.

"Everybody up!" he shouted. "We're going out!"

"Going out?" Beskaroon said, clearly eager for the action.

"Affirmative. A night mission."

Beskaroon glanced toward Sheba and muttered, "Just like the army. Spoil a fellow's best plans. Ah well, cutie, another night for us."

Sheba heard what he said but showed no understanding of it. Meanwhile, the squad made ready. Croft assembled his gear a little faster than usual, sure this had to be the night he would meet his death. Beskaroon, in battle readiness, came to Croft's bunk and said, "Sure you should go out, Croft? Been looking like death on a dry riverbed, you have."

"Stow it, Besky."

"Well, that's the Croft we know and love, anyway."

Beskaroon ambled away. For the first time in a long while a smile crossed Croft's face. The remark reminded him of the kind of comment Apollo would have made. He'd enjoyed it.

The squad crawled through a swamp. The musty unpleasant odor of the place seemed all around them. Everyone felt as if things were crawling on their skin, and there was a lot of quiet itching going on. Strange animal sounds that would have frightened most people did not faze them at all.

Beskaroon edged toward Sheba and whispered in her ear, "Tonight. When we get back. You and me, cutie. Send you into rapture, I will."

"Leave her alone, Besky," Xiomara said, laconically.

"Stay out of this, crudskin."

"Quiet," Barra ordered, "all of you."

Beskaroon got in one last whisper to Sheba, "Tonight."

Croft glanced toward Beskaroon and wondered if he should find a moment to polish Beskaroon off during the mission. Save Sheba some trouble. However attractive the idea was, it was not really Croft's style.

He was ready to consider it anyway when a loud explosion knocked the idea right out of his head. Looking behind him and up, he saw a figure sailing through the air. It was Sergeant Barra, his body twisted. Barra crashed to the ground. Croft crawled to him and saw that the new sergeant was dead.

Xiomara made her way to Croft and said, "What's happened?"

"I think we're in trouble."

Enemy guns opened fire on them. Squirming around in the swampy ground, they tried to shoot back. It was difficult to tell where the firing was coming from. What was sure was that they were pinned down. Laser beams lit up the night. Shots came close to the squad and made the damp ground seemed to sizzle, but so far no one but Barra had been hit.

"What should we do?" Sheba asked.

"All we can do is go the way we were going," Xiomara said.

"Where there's more of them waiting for us," Croft said. "We're trapped."

"Sounds like you've turned into a coward, Croft," Beskaroon said angrily.

"Just trying to emulate you, Besky."

"What do you mean?"

"Figure it out for yourself."

The squad kept returning fire, but it felt like shooting at ghosts. There was no indication they were hitting anything.

Suddenly there was a loud explosion and an enormous bright light. Croft shouted, "Stop firing! Look!"

When the squad stopped shooting, there was only quiet. The enemy attack had ended.

"They might be sneaking up on us," Xiomara said.

"Or trying to surround us," Beskaroon said.

"I'm not sure," Croft said warily. "Maybe we should—"

"Look!" cried Sheba.

There was movement ahead of them, dark shapes in the darkness. The squad gripped their weapons tighter and watched the apparitions come closer. The first ghost came into the light, and it was Apollo, waving to them. Behind him, the second phantom became Sarge.

Sheba shouted their names and ran to them. The others quickly followed. Sarge stood off to the side as Sheba, and then Xiomara, hugged Apollo. For his greeting, Croft tapped Apollo on the shoulder, then he asked, "What happened?"

"We've been tracking you since you left camp. When you were ambushed, we were practically standing next to your attackers. They were easy to wipe out. Only four guys with too many weapons."

In response to the questions of the squad, Apollo hastily explained what had happened to him and Sarge, and how they had come looking for the squad.

"We're all on the same side now," Apollo remarked.

"No, we ain't," Beskaroon said angrily. "Deserters, the both of you. Taking you in." He raised his pistol.

"No, listen," Apollo pleaded. "It's all because of the belt. The belt controls you."

"Nobody controls me," Beskaroon said. "I'm—"

"Show him, Sarge."

Heedless of Beskaroon's weapon, Sarge approached him.

Some of Sarge's former authority was still felt by Beskaroon, who backed away, shouting, "Sarge, I'll kill you. I'm not kidding."

He pointed the gun at Sarge's chest. Before he could fire, Xiomara shot the gun out of his hand. It flew a short distance, then landed with a splash in a puddle of swampy water. Before Beskaroon could do anything else, Sarge reached around him and manipulated the control stud, then he jerked the belt off Beskaroon. Reaching up to his forehead, he was able to remove the sweatband also.

Apollo worked the belt and sweatbands off Croft and Sheba while Sarge removed the control garments from Xiomara. When the quartet were freed of their belts and sweatbands, they felt dizzy for a while.

"You can actually feel it go, the grip on your mind," Xiomara said, awed. "I didn't realize I felt it."

"God," Croft said, fright in his voice, "a moment ago all I wanted was to get myself killed. I might have done it."

"Apollo," Sheba said, her voice trembling, "I tried to *kill* you!"

"I know," Apollo answered softly. "But not you really. The belt did it to you, turned you into a killer."

"But, if I had, it wouldn't've mattered about the belt. I would have—"

"Don't dwell on it. Anyway, we've got to get out of here. All the action might have alerted other units. What say, Sarge? Where should we go?"

"Back to the river. For now, anyway."

"My thinking exactly." He turned to address the others. "You'll like it there. It's peaceful, quiet."

"I could use a little peace and quiet right now," Sheba remarked.

"Well, it'll only be for a little while," Apollo said. "We've got work to do."

"You're kidding," Croft said. "Aren't you?"

"Not at all."

"No, I see you're not."

"Beskaroon?" Apollo said. "Staying? Or coming with us?"

Beskaroon seemed genuinely in doubt for a moment, then he said, "With you, Cap'n."

While the squad assembled its gear, Sarge walked slowly

over to Barra's corpse and looked down at him. Apollo came
to his side. Sarge addressed Apollo without looking at him.

"He was a good soldier. He shouldn't have died like this."

"No. None of 'em should."

"This war should end."

"Funny thing for you to say."

"I guess, in a way, the belt that controlled me is gone."

"Well, I did want to talk to you about the war and what to
do about it."

"Oh?"

"I have a plan."

"People like you always have plans. That's your curse, I
expect."

"I expect."

Apollo turned around, called to the squad, "Everyone ready?"

They all said yes and came to a kind of lazy attention. Apollo
turned back to Sarge and said, "Sarge, you lead the way. Your
job."

Sarge accepted the command easily. He was so used to
taking commands. This time, however, at least his officer wasn't
hiding behind the thick walls of a command bastion.

The squad trudged away, leaving behind them the swamp
and Barra's body.

CHAPTER TWENTY-FIVE

Adama and Starbuck were maneuvering their Vipers in precise formation, following a dictated search pattern. Starbuck was impressed at the Commander's skills. It must have been true, what they said. He must have been one real hotshot pilot.

They had just begun flying over Yevra, although they didn't know the planet by name. Starbuck activated his commline and spoke into it: "Just looks like another barren one, a copy of all the other planets in this system. And most of the other systems we've seen."

"I agree, Starbuck. This sub-sector seems totally devoid of any kind of life-forms. I can't detect—"

The way the Commander broke off made Starbuck look toward his Viper to make sure nothing had happened to it.

"What is it, sir?"

"I don't know, Starbuck. For a moment there, the scanner did a strange flip-flop, changed its readings almost entirely, then it returned to the same readings."

"A malfunction?"

"I suppose so. I'm going to descend a ways, take a closer look at this one."

"All right with me. I'll be right on your tail."

"Going down..."

Starbuck followed Adama's Viper. He was staring at it intently when it vanished from sight.

"What the—"

It made no sense. One moment the Commander's Viper was there, the next moment it was gone. He had to find him. He headed for the point where Adama's Viper had been.

"Commander A—"

The landscape below him seemed to magically transform itself, from barrenness to a lush richness.

The former Sweeper elite squad, including Beskaroon, crouched on a hilltop overlooking a strangely shaped fortification. It seemed built of odd-shaped blocks, with the sections shoved together randomly. It was made of thick stone and towered high in the sky.

The air was cool. It had recently rained and the stones and rocks they leaned against were still damp.

Apollo studied the fortification. There seemed to be no clear approaches to it, except for a heavily guarded roadway. He turned to Sarge, who was conducting the same surveillance right next to him.

"That it?" Apollo asked.

"That is the Sweeper's command bastion. The bastion for the Pelters is located some distance from here, nearly on the other side of Yevra."

Croft, sitting on the other side of Sarge, whistled and said, "And we're supposed to get in *there?*"

"I didn't promise easy work," Sarge said. "But, after all, we are ingeniously trained, all of us."

"And where would our Vipers be?" Apollo asked.

"I can't say. On the roof, I would suspect, if they could get them there. Even if they couldn't fly them, they could use cargo aircraft to lift them up there. Their own less efficient planes take off and land on the roof. But they may have been taken elsewhere for research and examination."

"Well," Apollo remarked, "whatever we do, we should at least get a clue to where they are. Best we can do."

"Many victories have been based on such anomalous factors," Sarge said, aware he was sounding again like a training noncom.

"And many more defeats," Croft added.

Sheba, on the other side of Apollo, commented, "Good to see that Croft has regained his cantankerous spirit, don't you think?"

"I'll show you cantankerous, Sheba," Croft said.

"Look forward to it," Sheba said.

Apollo was pleased by the good-natured feeling that Croft and Sheba exhibited in their bantering. It was a significant contrast to their recent behavior. He turned again to Sarge, asking, "We should wait? Wait and observe?"

"Yes. There'll be an opportunity. I suspect their security is less than effective. Nobody's tried to attack a bastion in so long they won't be expecting anything, especially a small force like ours."

"Our advantage."

They kept watch on the fortress for a long while. Not much happened. A vehicle like the one Apollo had traveled in with Tren landed on the roof. Some soldiers marched in file along the roadway and into the bastion.

Apollo crawled over to Xiomara, who was doing her surveillance from a different angle.

"See anything?" he asked.

"Nothing useful."

He touched the back of her tunic. His hand caressed in a slow circle, feeling a certain tactile familiarity with what was beneath the cloth.

"You don't have to do that," Xiomara said without looking at him.

"I want to."

"Apollo, I'm quite happy with last night. I enjoyed it. But you have no obligations to me."

"I know that. I just—"

"Want to take me home and introduce me to your father, the Commander?"

"Yes. Yes, I would."

She laughed.

"Maybe you would. Don't worry, I won't go. But it's nice to know you would take me. Face like this, I don't go seeking anyone's society."

"We have medical facilities, amazing ones. We could do something for you, perhaps."

"For this? This doesn't come off with surgery. It is bound

to me and can't be altered. Not by medical treatment, anyway. I don't even mind it anymore. There are bigger matters to consider. How to restore my home, my planet. How to end this stupid war."

Apollo gazed across at the bastion. It seemed so impenetrable. He wondered how they'd ever find their way into its interior. They might crouch on this hilltop forever.

After Adama had flown through the force field, he was astonished by the drastic changes in the surfaces below him. The new beautiful landscape stretched almost from horizon to horizon. In the distance the horizon seemed to stop much sooner than it should. That was a sign, he figured, of the presence of a force field, one that camouflaged the loveliness of the planet by projecting above it the contours of a barren land. Making a loop, he saw the smoke and flame of a battle far away.

"Lieutenant Starbuck!" he shouted and got no answer. "Starbuck, answer me, where are you?"

He scanned the skies for Starbuck's Viper. Suddenly it materialized quite close to him and he heard Starbuck's anxious voice: "—dama, Commander . . . I see you, Commander. What's going on? What happened down there?"

"We've just flown through a wall of some kind of force field used to camouflage the real planet. It's not designed to keep us out, but merely disguise the landscape so that no one will try to land under ordinary conditions."

"Do you think Apollo might have come here then?"

"It's a possibility. Remember Omega saying that the ships seemed to vanish from the scanner screen? That could be because they went through this force field. Our telemetry might have been able to record only what is transmitted from here."

"Transmitted? By whom?"

"That's what we'll try to find out. Set your telemetry to locate Vipers."

"Aye, aye, sir."

"We'll fly circle patterns, staying close but covering as much area as we can."

"Yes, sir."

Starbuck was impressed by the energy in Adama's voice. He sounded like a young pilot. It was a pleasure to be flying as his wingmate.

• • •

The flat vehicle with the canopy was rising again from the roof. It hovered above the roof for a moment and Apollo could see two soldiers inside the transparent canopy.

"I wonder..." he mused.

"What?" Sarge asked.

"Do you think we could all fit on one of those? More important, would it carry our combined weight? And could we figure out how to fly it? Tren used a control, I can just remember. Look, it's coming our way. How convenient."

"You going to jump up and snag it, Apollo?" Croft said.

"Not exactly."

He left the shelter of his rock and waved at the vehicle, which began to descend toward Apollo.

"That's a ship?" Croft whispered. "It looks more like a rug. Why are you waving to it?"

"Keep still, Croft."

The two soldiers inside the canopy stared at Apollo quizzically. One was reptilian, the other humanoid. Puzzled or not, they were nevertheless landing the ship. As the canopy went up and tipped back, the two soldiers stepped forward, brandishing weapons.

"Take it easy, guys," Apollo said. "We need help. A wounded sergeant. Sarge?"

Improvising, Sarge limped into sight and said in a croaking voice: "We were ambushed, we—"

Apollo made his move, jumping the reptilian soldier and wrenching the weapon out of his hand. Sarge took care of the other, knocking him unconscious with one smooth punch. Croft stood up, saying, "Now what?"

"We take a trip to the castle there."

"In *that*," Beskaroon said, pointing to the ship.

"There isn't enough room for all of us," Croft said.

"Well, that is a logistics problem," Apollo said. "But it's almost nightfall, and I think we can pull it off. Meantime, let's get these two characters trussed up."

Confused, Croft and Beskaroon nevertheless began tying up their two captives.

In a large control room inside the bastion, two officers crouched in front of a large scanner console. Both were reptiles and looked amazingly like Sarge. They had just detected the presence in their skies of the Vipers of Adama and Starbuck, and were tracking them.

"They're nowhere near here yet," one officer said.

"But the precise pattern they seem to be flying will bring them to this vicinity soon," said the other.

"We must be ready, just in case. Call an alert."

"Yes, sir."

"We'll wipe them out of the sky if we have to." Returning his attention to the screen, the first officer muttered, "Interesting."

"What's interesting, sir?"

"These intruders. Their vehicles are exact matches for the ones we captured. I'd like to get these, too, but I think, under the circumstances, it will be safer to blow them up."

"I agree, sir."

Adama and Starbuck continued their pattern. It took them over the battle Adama had detected earlier. They took some time to study it.

"What do you think, Starbuck?"

"It all looks pretty primitive to me. Some kind of local war. Nothing we can interfere in, at any rate."

"Right. Look at them, though. Such a trivial thing, war."

"I don't usually hear it described as trivial, sir."

"Compared to what we've been through, that little brushfire affair down there doesn't amount to a hill of felgercarb. We lost twelve entire worlds, Starbuck. Those people down there are probably fighting over small pieces of land. Why can't people work out their differences?"

"An old dilemma, Commander."

"From an old man, Starbuck."

"Right-o."

They put the battle behind them. Since they were heading for the dark side of the planet, they would have to rely on their telemetry even more.

"Commander!" Starbuck cried out suddenly. "I've detected something. Not far from here. Some kind of large structure on a mountain."

"Let's head for it."

"I'm with you."

• • •

The two officers inside the bastion observed the course change of the pair of Vipers and realized the aircraft was heading right for the bastion now.

"Alert the battery. We'll fire when they're close."

"Yes, sir."

The Sweeper flying vehicle was halfway between the hilltop and the bastion. It flew over a deep valley. A long fall. Sarge was in the canopy, steering the vehicle, with Sheba and Xiomara squeezed in beside him. Clutching the flat narrow sides of the vehicle, their bodies dangling downward, their legs swinging, were Apollo, Croft and Beskaroon. Croft shouted to Apollo, "Captain, I want to be frank with you, I'm not comfortable."

"C'mon, Croft," Apollo yelled back. "You love this kind of derring-do. Remember on Tairac? You swung from a Viper into another aircraft to save Boxey."

"I was out of my mind."

"But you saved him. And I had to thank you, remember?"

"Must have been painful for you. We certainly have had an up-and-down relationship since."

"You intend that as a pun?"

"Sure."

Beskaroon, confused by the banter of the two odd men, growled, "Can't figure you guys at all. Talk funny, you do. Strange, strange."

"Don't let it put strain on your brain cell, Besky," Croft said.

Off to their left the sky lit up. A large wide beam of light scanning the sky had come on near the roof of the fortress. Their small vehicle was out of its present range.

"What's that?" Apollo said. "They can't have spotted us."

"Maybe they're looking for us. Can't we get this thing moving any faster?"

"Only if you drop away."

Apollo continued to stare at the light, even though its brightness hurt his eyes. Suddenly he saw what it was aimed at as two vehicles flew into the light.

"It's Vipers!" he yelled. "From the *Galactica*."

"What the hell are they doing here?" Croft said.

"I don't know, but we've got to contact them."

"If those guys don't shoot 'em down first."

"Look down there, Croft. On the roof. It's our ships."

A benefit of the searchlight was that it also lit up the fortress roof. Resting there, one of them partially dismantled, were the stolen spacecraft.

As the Sweeper vehicle, guided surely by Sarge, started to make its descent, the guns inside the bastion opened fire on Adama and Starbuck's Vipers. Apollo twisted his head around to look. One shot came dangerously near one of the Vipers, which swerved just in time. It looked like the Sweeper artillery might be too slow for a Viper. Both Vipers eased into an upward turn. The artillery, having made an adjustment for the move, fired again. Again their aim was just off the mark.

In their Vipers, Adama and Starbuck were manipulating their controls furiously.

"What's going on?" Starbuck said. "They fire at all strange aircraft here, without trying to find out what—"

"Remember there's a war going on here. They see us as a threat. Let's get out of their way. Evasive maneuver."

"Roger."

The next shot came so close that Adama could almost feel it creating a sizzle along the side of his Viper.

As the Sweeper vehicle neared the roof's surface, Apollo and Croft jumped down and began to run. Beskaroon followed a couple of beats later. Sarge landed the craft smoothly and flipped up the canopy. Xiomara and Sheba were on the run, their weapons ready.

Ahead of them there were only a couple of defenders, both of whom were so astonished by the force charging at them they were slow to react. Xiomara dropped one and Apollo took care of the other. Gathering the group next to the dismantled Viper, with his eye on the Vipers in the sky, he spoke quickly: "Sarge, you and the others are to follow the original plan—do anything you can to take care of the bastion. Sheba, you and I're going to take the two good Vipers here up, link up with the others, try to mount an air attack on this damn place. All that okay with you, Croft?"

Croft, glad to be consulted, said, "You two are the best pilots and, anyway, you're the boss, Appy."

"Appy? Sheba asked, confused.

"Affectionate nickname," Croft said, smiling.

Apollo ignored the comment and shouted, "Let's go!"

He and Sheba headed for the Vipers while the others searched for a way into the fortress.

"What is it, Starbuck?"

"Something on telemetry. I don't know, I could swear . . . but—"

"Spit it out, Starbuck!"

"I think it's Vipers. They're taking off from the roof of that building. You think they're friendly?"

Adama examined the configurations on his own screen and said softly, "Well, they're our ships. But be ready to fire at them, just in case."

"Right."

The way the ships flew so directly at them they seemed threatening. Adama's thumb lightly touched the top of his fire button. Apollo's voice on his commline made him draw back his thumb abruptly.

"This is Captain Apollo of the *Battlestar Galactica*. Do you read me?"

"Read you, Apollo," said Starbuck in an impossibly joy-filled voice. "Like a book I read you, good buddy."

"Starbuck! Shoulda known it was you. And who's the hotshot in the other Viper?"

Adama almost choked with laughter as he said, "It's your hotshot father, Apollo."

The subsequent silence on the commline seemed loud with Apollo's shock.

"Father! What? How?"

"We'll get to that information later. More important, Apollo, where have you been? What's going on? Who's with you?"

"Sublieutenant Sheba, sir."

"And Croft? Is he okay?"

"He's down there," Apollo replied. "With the others."

"The others?"

"I'll explain as fast as I can. We have to attack."

Sarge led the way down the corridor. Croft thought he'd never seen so many interlocking corridors with so few personnel

roaming them. They had been able to dispense easily with each
Sweeper they encountered.

Sarge gestured his reduced elite squad to a halt and said,
"The war room is through that door, the battery on the other
side of it. If we disrupt the war room, that'll help Apollo and
the others in their air assault on the fortification. Might wipe
out the resistance altogether."

"Let's take it!" Croft said eagerly.

"There may be a hundred officers in the war room," Sarge
cautioned.

"Just the kinds of odds I like."

"Well..."

"Sit it out, Sarge, if you like. I understand. They're your
side, after all. But we've got a chance here to screw up this
war for good, I want to take it."

"Yes, I do, too. But four of us against a hundred?"

"There's no choice. And the Vipers'll be back momentarily.
That particular diversion should decrease the odds consider-
ably."

"*If* the Vipers come back..."

"What're you two jawin' about?" Beskaroon growled.

"Nothing," Sarge answered. "On the count of three, we're
going in there. Everyone ready? Good. One, two, three..."

As a unit, almost like the elite squad of days gone by, the
four warriors charged forward and crashed through the war-
room door.

Inside the war room the pair of commanding officers continued to track the flights of the Vipers. They had not yet gotten
over their confusion when two of their Vipers had taken off to
join the other two.

"The strange aircraft, they are returning."

"Do you think they will attack?"

"Definitely."

"We will shoot them out of the skies this—"

Suddenly the door at the far end of the war room crashed
open. The air was so suddenly filled with weaponsfire that the
officers had no idea of the size of the assault force. But they
did see several fires suddenly erupt on equipment all around
the room. Many of their colleagues had already fallen. The
attack had been such a surprise that little resistance had so far

been offered. The invaders had taken up strategic positions behind destroyed equipment.

"What should we do?" one officer said.

"Our duty. We must guide the attack on the aircraft. Leave this little ambush to others."

"Little? Doesn't look little. Nobody's ever attacked a command bastion before, from the air or inside. Now we've got both!"

"There are many facets to war. Let us retreat to the battery room, to guide our guns in demolishing the air attack."

Crouching, they slipped through the battle and through the door to the battery room.

The Vipers closed on the bastion. Apollo had just finished explaining the situation to Adama and Starbuck.

"Then we should attack immediately?" Adama asked.

"That's the plan."

"All right with you, Starbuck?"

"I'm ready."

"You lead the way, Apollo."

"Yes, sir!"

The sweeper officers carefully watched the quartet of Vipers come closer. When they seemed securely in the battery's gunsights, an officer shouted for them to fire. They had not been aware of the Vipers' capacity for maneuverability. Although the shots would have been true for the kind of aircraft the Sweeper officers understood, they merely whizzed by the rapidly dodging Vipers. However, one shot did come extremely close to the tip of Starbuck's canopy.

"Try to part my hair, willya?" he shouted. "Okay for you, whoever you are."

He flew in dangerously close to the bastion itself, managing to slip under the lines of fire of the Sweeper guns. With a sure thumb on the firing button, he let off a series of shots that created a big hole around one cannon. First parts of the wall fell away, then the big gun shifted forward and slid easily through the new hole. It seemed to drift slowly to the ground, where it crashed heavily and broke into several pieces.

The Sweeper officers tried to rouse the remaining gunners, but the ghostly-looking creatures whitened further in fear. One officer shoved a whole team back to its gun. When they were ready to fire again, the door behind them crashed open and the four warriors of the attack force rushed in.

They wiped out the rest of the battery in a moment, and Beskaroon screamed with glee as he ran across the room, still firing.

"Nice shooting, Sarge," Croft said, relaxing.

"Nothing nice about it. It's why I'm a good soldier."

Croft smiled.

"I just love that sort of crap, Sarge. The dedicated soldier and all that. Take it on the road."

"I don't understand. It's true, isn't it?"

"Doesn't matter."

Sarge decided to ignore Croft's odd comments. He was too interested in his own acts during this battle. He had not been concerned at first. He had merely functioned as a soldier. Then he had killed the two commanding officers of the bastion. Such an act was against all his training, but he was not remorseful. He did, after all, understand his choices and their consequences. He merely regretted the necessity of it.

"Those ships," Beskaroon cried. "They're landing on the roof."

"We better get upstairs," Croft said. "Be the welcoming party for the hotshots."

They started out the door, Xiomara leading the way. As Croft came through after her, he saw a sudden motion off to his left. A Sweeper officer appeared from behind a pile of debris, his gun poised. He saw Xiomara first and, loyal to the last, took his shot at her. She doubled up and fell to the floor.

"Xiomara!" Croft had warned, but a fraction too late. He shot quickly, catching the ambusher in the neck and sending him reeling backwards, dead. Croft knelt down by Xiomara.

"Are you all right?" he said. He could not tell from her face whether she was in pain, or even conscious.

"I . . . doubt it," she answered.

He looked up at Beskaroon and shouted, "Besky! Get Apollo! Bring him here."

Beskaroon pushed past them and ran out the war-room door. Croft tended to Xiomara while Sarge scouted the room, making sure there were no more survivors about to take potshots. In a moment, Apollo came rushing in, his face fearful, shouting, "Xiomara!"

"I . . . don't think there's . . . anything you can do, hero. This feels pretty bad. More than bad."

"Let me see."

Apollo took Croft's place next to her. Even as he checked the wound, which was bloody and raw around the edges, he got a flash of Serina lying wounded on the planet Kobol. Working on Xiomara now seemed like re-experience of that time. He had only been able to keep Serina alive until they reached the *Galactica*. He had to do better with Xiomara.

"It might not have damaged vital organs, Xiomara," he said soothingly.

"Don't kid me. Something hurts bad in there. I don't know what, but—"

"Don't waste your energy talking. Let's see what I can do."

Trying to staunch the blood flow, he thought of how he'd believed he'd failed when Serina had died. He had felt massive guilt then and nobody had been able to convince him that her death was not his fault. He didn't want to face that guilt again, after Xiomara. She must be saved.

"Apollo," Xiomara said abruptly.

"I told you to keep still."

"I don't do what people tell me. Apollo, thank you. You were very nice to me. I liked that."

"Had nothing to do with being nice."

"Don't be such a hero, hero. Be yourself. Be—"

She groaned loudly.

"Something hurt?" Apollo asked, trying to sound like a proper doctor.

"You . . . might . . . say . . . that."

Her eyes closed. Her chest heaved once and then she seemed to stop breathing. Apollo pushed at it, screaming, "Xiomara, no!"

"Apollo," she whispered, without seeming to take another breath, as if the word was the last she could push through with the air she had left.

"No, I won't—"

He was trying to say he wouldn't allow her to die, but he couldn't finish the sentence. He watched her face become peaceful as life seemed to leave it. Then the face, its outlines always shimmery, became ghostlike and ethereal. Gradually its awful features seemed to dissolve, slowly revealing underneath, as if by a lifting of the ugly mask, a lovely face. Pale and sad, but lovely. It was the face Apollo had glimpsed for an instant several times. Her eyes where shut and her hair was in disarray, but the rest of the face was not only beautiful and sculptured but also breathtaking. High cheekbones, clear skin, a delicate nose, lovely lips, a strange peaceful smile.

"My God!" Croft whispered. "That's what . . . what she really looks like!"

"I don't understand," Beskarron said in an almost whiny voice. "That ugly thing . . . looks like that? What is it, some kind of magic, some—"

"Shut up, Besky," Croft muttered angrily.

They all stared at the apparition of incredible beauty. Even Sarge, who could not perceive it, was fascinated by the magical change itself. He recognized, too, that the peace in the face was a definite contrast to the way the old face had been twisted in pain. An already twisted face, twisted in pain.

Apollo's whisper was faint but firm, anguished but calm. "Xiomara, don't die. Do not die."

He remembered the time he had seemed to die, remembered that apparent death was not necessarily final. There were miracles. He whispered again for her not to die. For a moment the real face appeared to shimmer as the old one had, as if in response to Apollo's invocation. Then suddenly, noisily, with a great choking sound, Xiomara took a breath, and the movement of her chest up and down became normal. As her breathing returned, her old face slowly returned, in the reverse of the stages by which it disappeared. When the face was complete, her eyes came open.

"What happened?" she said. "There was light and—"

"Don't try to talk. We've got to get you out of here, treat you. Sarge!"

"Yes!"

"You have any of those herbs with you?"

"Yes, I kept some. You think they'll work on her?"

"It's worth a try. They worked on you, didn't they? Give them to me."

Sarge quickly removed the greenish-blue herbs from his sidepack but, instead of giving them to Apollo, he pushed the captain aside and began to tend to Xiomara's wound himself.

CHAPTER TWENTY-SIX

Xiomara came awake suddenly. She felt perspiration drying on her face, some discomfort at the center of her body. She knew that she had been out for a long while this time. At other times she had come to brief consciousness to find various members of the elite squad tending to her. Apollo, Sheba, Croft, Sarge, even Beskaroon. Beskaroon had, in fact, said something nice to her. She couldn't recall what it was.

Apollo walked into her line of vision and smiled down at her.

"Good to see you awake," he said. "Now I know you'll be all right."

"Just because I'm awake?" she asked, her voice weak.

"Well, I was beginning to worry you might slip into a coma. Your wound is healing fine. Just fine."

She glanced down and saw that the wound had been efficiently taken care of and lightly bandaged. She took a deep breath. The discomfort around the wound increased but was bearable.

"I do remember being shot, and you tending to me, and

then a bright light, and then everything all confused, and then little else. Except I came awake a few times in this room. Where am I?"

"You're still in the command bastion of the Sweepers. We're the only ones here now. It's sort of been our base."

"Base?"

"Well, that's a long story. I'll get to it."

"You'll tell me now. I'm all right."

Apollo settled down on the edge of the bed. He told her how they'd found this medical facility in a lower floor of the bastion. They'd brought her here and been taking care of her ever since.

"That's kind of you, all of you."

"Nothing to it. There's someone here I'd like you to meet."

He gestured to someone on the other side of Xiomara's bed. A young blond man came into view, smiling self-consciously.

"Xiomara, this is Starbuck. The real Starbuck."

"Seem to be a lot of fake Starbucks around," Starbuck said amiably.

"Apollo told us stories about you."

"Yeah, he told me. But whatever he said, don't you believe a word. He told me he made up the stories."

"Oh, I know that. We all knew that. He was trying to keep up our spirits. We knew you couldn't have done all he said you did."

"I'm crushed. Maybe there was *some* truth in them. Anyway, I just wanted to say hello. The Commander's got me over-hauling the Vipers. I'll see you soon, Xiomara. Up and around."

With a small good-bye wave, Starbuck left the room.

"Your friend seems very nice," Xiomara said, looking after him.

"He is."

"What's all that about working on the Vipers?"

"Well, they got pretty damaged."

"Oh, in the attack on this bastion."

"Not just that, actually. You've been out for a while. See, after the battle here was over, we realized that we'd left the war wide open for the other side to win. Without anyone guiding the movements of the Sweepers from this bastion, the Pelters—whoever they are—would just overwhelm the others, and perhaps thousands would be killed in the process. So, Croft, Sheba, Starbuck, my father and I each took a Viper and attacked the command bastion of the Pelters, which is on the other side of Yevra. Funny, it's almost as if the two sides set up their command posts as two ends of a game board."

"What's funny? As far as I've seen, this war is a game for both sides."

"A game?"

"Did they want this land? Was there any wealth on Yevra for them to win? Would they gain any power by ravaging Yevra with their awful battles? I don't know what the original reasons for this war were—"

"Nobody does apparently."

"—but it looks like the war became a thing to be conducted for itself, and for none of the other reasons that war usually comes from."

"I think you're right. You should have been a general, Xiomara."

Her response was unusually firm, even when spoken in her weakened voice: "No. I don't want to have anything to do with war again."

"Well, Yevra won't have to suffer anymore because of *this* war. Once we'd destroyed both bastions, we flew over a battle and were actually able to watch it slow to a standstill. Soon soldiers were wandering around aimlessly, not sure of what they were supposed to be. Both sides got mixed up together and looked like one army that couldn't find another army to fight. Last I checked, most of the soldiers had wandered off. To more peaceful pursuits, I hope. Or to find a way back to their original homes. Beskaroon has already located some of his former crew."

"Beskaroon. He was in here."

"Well, he and Sarge couldn't go up in the Vipers and, while we were attending to the Pelter command post, they did a lot of the tending to you. Actually, Beskaroon did most of it, Sarge says. Sarge had to check out every nook and cranny of this building to make sure we were in no more danger. So Beskaroon was your primary nurse."

"Not willingly, I'm sure."

"Willingly," Beskaroon said. He had been hiding in the shadows of a corner of the room. "Thought you were a brave woman, I did. Sorry I was a lout. Always a lout, that's me. Forgiveness may be given, please."

"I forgive you."

Beskaroon seemed quite happy as he exited the room. Apollo suggested to Xiomara that she get some more rest, and he started to follow Beskaroon out the door.

"Apollo?" Xiomara said.

"Yes?"

"What are your plans?"

"Plans?"

"I suspect you don't plan to take up residence on Yevra."

Apollo turned, clearly hesitant to discuss this particular subject. He sat again on the side of her bed.

"I'll return to the *Galactica*. Soon. I've thought about you a lot, Xiomara. You could return with us. We could consult Doctor Salik, our medical officer, see if something can be done about . . . about your looks."

"Don't be afraid to say face. I think, Apollo, the spell is too strong. I was told there was nothing physical that can be done, and I believe that. I don't think your doctor can counteract that kind of power."

"Xiomara—"

"I can't even give it a try. I must find someone here, on Yevra, who can do something. There is no cure for me on the *Galactica*."

"I have to return there, Xiomara."

"I know that."

"And you won't come."

"No. There are things to do here. Villages to restore, life to bring back to normal. I'll stay for that. I can be helpful. The training we received from Sarge has benefits for peacetime. But I'll think of you often, hero. And don't worry, I wouldn't have gone to your ship with you even if I had my normal face."

"Why?"

"I don't love you, Apollo. I love Trelon. I will look for him. Perhaps he didn't die in the war."

Apollo took her hand, held it tight.

"I hope Trelon's alive."

"Thank you. And thanks for . . . everything, hero."

He released his grip on her hand and stood up.

"I didn't do anything."

"But yes, you did. You looked at me, really looked at me. I liked that. I will miss you."

"I'll miss you, too."

They stared at each for a long while, neither of them able to think of anything more to say. Apollo, saying he had duty to attend to, said good-bye and walked to the door.

"By the way," Xiomara called after him, "you didn't love me either."

"No, I guess I didn't. I'm not sure."

"Thank you again then. For being uncertain."

Apollo left without looking back at her. She lay back on her bed, wanting to go to sleep again. Her eyes shut, she touched her face with her fingertips, traced its contours, then she bit the back of her hand, to keep from crying.

CHAPTER TWENTY-SEVEN

Adama leaned against his Viper and enjoyed the slightly oily smells that rose up from its surface. He almost regretted the fact that they were returning to the *Galactica*. The responsible side of him longed to get back there, feel the power of the helm, and continue the quest. But the small hotshot-pilot side of him wouldn't have minded a few more air battles. He had enjoyed the pair of combat missions he'd been part of. Even more than being in the saddle again, he had liked flying side by side with his son. He had never expected that particular bonus. He could still feel the thrill that had gone through them after they had defeated the Pelter command bastion and had made the wide turn to go back. He had looked over at Apollo's Viper and caught Apollo smiling over at him. The warmth of that moment would do him good for many centons to come.

Now he had only to wait for the good-byes to be said. He had already bade his farewell to the strange beings who had become his son's new friends. Apollo now spoke to Sarge. The odd-looking but compelling and brave woman called Xiomara stood nearby, waiting for Sarge and Apollo to finish. Apollo had told his father about Xiomara, how she had become such a grotesque creature, and what she had done in battle. Adama had detected beneath Apollo's words a more-than-ordinary interest in the woman, and a sadness that she had refused to accompany them to the *Galactica*.

Starbuck, who had also said his good-byes, stood next to Adama.

"Strange," the young lieutenant said, wistfully.

"What's strange, Starbuck?"

"What we've done here. We've liberated a planet we never heard of before. I mean, we came in here like trained mercenaries, knowing nothing about the conflict, and took care of it."

"Not exactly mercenaries, Starbuck. After all, we took no one side."

"Yes, we demolished both sides equally. Oh, I know it was for the good of the planet and all that, but it just feels strange. I never fought a battle before where I didn't know something about the issues involved."

"Apollo says there were no real issues. It was a war fought for the sake of the war itself."

"Yeah, but I can't quite grasp that. You did prove yourself a real hotshot, though, Commander."

"Really, Starbuck, I don't think . . ."

"Hey, if there were a Hotshot Hall of Fame, the bust of you would be right up front, I'm sure."

Adama grimaced and said, "God, Starbuck, I hope not."

"I wish you a safe trip to your home ship," Sarge said.

"Thank you, Sarge," Apollo said. "What are you going to do now?"

"I'll find my way to my own home, my own planet. Eventually."

"Eventually?"

"There is some work I feel I should do here. I am well trained. There are ways I can help to restore Yevra to its former state."

"And then you'll go?"

"Then I'll go."

"I wish I could take you with us. We need brave warriors on the *Galactica*."

"I am no longer a warrior. I would not be comfortable on your ship."

"I wish you could be, but I understand. Well, what do you

do in your culture to display a fond farewell to a comrade?"

"We are not demonstrative. We merely say farewell."

"Then farewell, Sarge."

"Farewell, Apollo."

Sarge showed no emotion as he turned and walked away from Apollo, yet Apollo was certain the reptilian creature had felt something. He wanted to run after Sarge, embrace him or shake his hand, but he couldn't risk offending him.

Croft and Sheba strolled to their Vipers.

"I'll be glad to get off this place," Croft said.

"I don't know. It's going to be pleasant here now, once it's restored to its former—"

"Nah. There're always gonna be the scars of war all around. On the landscape, the rubble of old villages, the scars inside. Yevra will never be the same. They may figure out ways to start new wars."

"The old cynicism, huh? At least it shows you're back to normal, Croft."

"And speaking of back to normal, when we get back to the *Galactica*, I'd like for us to share a bottle of Ambrosa and exchange old war stories."

"Well, you just stare into your drink and, if you see me there, start talking."

Croft smiled. The old Sheba seemed to be back, too. He was tempted to put his arm around her. He knew it would annoy her, and he liked that. But, for once, he decided against annoying someone. Instead, they walked silently, Croft sneaking looks at Sheba's profile. It was lovely, he thought, the way her features complemented her large eyes. He wondered if he could change his ways for her. He doubted it.

Apollo had trouble finding words to say to Xiomara.

"Then you know where to look for Trelon?"

"I think so. At least as near as I can figure with the records I found in the bastion's file room. I know his last assignment anyway."

"I hope you find him. And I . . . I hope you . . ."

He couldn't figure a way to phrase what he wanted to say, so she said it for him, "Find a way to get rid of this face? Maybe I will. Believe me, Apollo, I am frightened of the day when I do find Trelon. What if I'm wrong about him, or what if he's changed by the war? He might take one look at this face and run."

"I don't think so."

She looked off toward the horizon, herself unable to speak for a moment. She finally said, "It'll be enough to know he's alive. If he doesn't want me, well . . ."

"He'll want you."

For a long while they stood awkwardly, in silence, then Xiomara said, "Well, your friends and your father are all assembled. Go quickly."

"Xiomara . . ."

"Don't say it. So long, hero."

Apollo moved toward her instead of away. She started to wave him back but was not successful. He took her in his arms and kissed her. As they separated he smiled at her tenderly, then turned abruptly and ran to his Viper.

Soon all of the pilots were in their cockpits. At an order from Adama they taxied into formation and then quickly took off. The Vipers sailed upward, turned in formation, and passed over Xiomara, who kept her eyes fixed upon them. They flew upward and vanished into the upper atmosphere.

For a moment Xiomara was not sure of what to do, where to start. Then she was aware of someone standing beside her. She turned and saw Beskaroon. She wondered if she was in danger from him now that the others had gone.

"Ready, are you?" he asked.

"For . . . for what?"

"Going to help you find your, what is his name, Trelzin, we are."

"Trelon."

"Yeah, Trelon. More help you can get, sooner you can find him."

"You said we?"

"Yep. He's gonna help, too—Sarge. Hey, Sarge! You comin'?"

As they watched Sarge amble toward them, Xiomara had a sudden memory of an event that had occurred the previous day. Apollo had been showing her his Viper, explaining how it worked. He had cleaned and polished it, and it shone brightly. As he talked on about controls and maneuverability, she caught sight of herself reflected on the Viper's surface. Her face was lovely, perhaps it had never been lovelier. She wanted to interrupt Apollo, point to her image, then she had realized he would not see that image. It had saddened her briefly, but she had been able to ignore the reflection for the rest of Apollo's explanation.

Now Sarge joined Xiomara and Beskaroon and silently they started in the direction of the place that bastion records had indicated as Trelon's last posting. Xiomara wondered if an outsider would have considered them a strange trio. A man who was clearly an oafish lout, a lizardlike being still in his sergeant's uniform, and a woman with a deformed face. Ah, what did it matter what an outsider thought?

Soon they were walking down a wide road. They passed many dazed refugees of the war. Sarge had to stop every few steps for Xiomara and Beskaroon to catch up.

MORE SCIENCE FICTION ADVENTURE!